FATHER IS PLEASED

L. Andrew Cooper

Horrific Scribblings, LLC, North Hollywood, CA, USA

CONTENTS

FOREWORD

To the Curious Reader:

I finished the manuscript of *Father Is Pleased* months before my own father died and can say with certainty that my own father had nothing to do with the inspiration for this story or the "Father" character(s) in it. The relationship between Felix and Father does involve a dark and twisted version of feelings involved in father-son bonding (among other things), and Father might raise questions about demagoguery, patriarchy, and paternalism, but rereading the story in the aftermath of my own father's death doesn't strike any chords for me related to personal Daddy issues.

Nevertheless, the basic idea of publishing a story with this content and this title that revolves around someone called "Father" so soon after my own father's death is weird. But I never said I'm not weird.

This story does get me now on a more personal and emotional level with what it reveals about the beliefs of Father's following. I struggle with nihilism, so the idea of living according to systematized nihilism—while it fascinates me enough to write about it—frightens me profoundly. I hope you feel at least somewhat the same. You'll enjoy the book more.

Darkly devoted,

L. Andrew Cooper
North Hollywood, California
May 7, 2025

WARNING

Father is Pleased is a work of extreme horror. It is intended for a mature audience. It contains graphic violence, explicit sexuality, sexual violence, profanity, and other potentially triggering or controversial material that some readers might find unsuitable.

1. THE DIRT CIRCLE

Huge-o drove his elbow into the left side of Felix's jaw, sending bolts of pain throughout his face, into his eye, and around his skull. Felix staggered backward, vision blurry, tripped on his own foot, and fell on his ass. Upon impact, he bit his lower lip and felt blood squirt around his mouth. Sitting down made Huge-o look more huge, all seven feet of him, torso and shoulders like stacks of cinderblocks, legs and arms a variety of barrels held together by sturdy ropes. Felix had always called him simply Hugo, but the younger kids called him "Huge-o" to his face, and now the audience around the circle chanted: "HUGE-O! HUGE-O! HUGE-O!" Size and a good nickname made him popular.

If Felix didn't get up, Huge-o could hammer the top of Felix's head, knock him senseless, seize the advantage. Father watched. Felix had to move. He scurried back, got traction with his bare feet in the yellow dirt, and stood as Huge-o, slow as his name suggested, lunged and missed. Felix hopped to a more distant part of the circle, spat out blood, and ignored the pain of smiling. "Missed your chance, huh?"

"Not in a hurry," Huge-o said.

People around the circle who could hear Huge-o laughed, but Hugo's answer wasn't bravado. Hugo didn't want to kill Felix, and Felix didn't want to kill him. Felix had been a presumptive contestant since he'd turned eighteen six months ago and been named, but he'd had to wait for a rival. Felix and Hugo weren't close friends, but they were friends, and Hugo's birthday wasn't far enough behind Felix's for them not to worry. First, another boy raised in the Lands turned eighteen but wasn't found worthy. Then another boy came of age, same thing. Nobody was surprised when Huge-o Hugo was named on his eighteenth birthday. The contest was set.

The flesh must be torn.

Felix didn't want to kill Hugo, but he felt destined to be a True Son, and Father watched.

Huge-o closed in on Felix's new position as Felix bounced on his toes, building energy and momentum. Felix had attended every contest he was allowed to witness and studied many others. The fights usually began with wrestling, the young men using their full bodies to negotiate control, and then dissolved into chaotic thrashing. Choke holds were forbidden. Strangulation for more than a three-count brought devastating lashes from the Monitor, a woman in a leather mask who stood at the circle's edge with her whip ready. Felix wasn't supposed to know she was Kate, a teacher at the school.

The flesh must be torn.

Instead of wrestling, in which Huge-o might have quickly overpowered Felix due to the weight difference—Felix was a little under six feet and only weighed about one sixty despite an athletic build—Huge-o had started in a street-boxing stance, with such a tight guard that Felix couldn't have grappled him down into the dirt if he'd wanted to. Boxing, though, opened up a venerable strategy for the little guy: tire the big guy out. When Huge-o stopped to catch his breath, Felix could beat the shit out of him.

Huge-o swung his left fist. Felix dodged. Huge-o tried a right hook. Felix dodged, saw an opening, jabbed Huge-o in the stomach, and jumped back. Coughing, Huge-o swung with the right again. Felix didn't even have to dodge.

They were naked. Everyone in the Lands followed cleansing regimens for diet and exercise, so everyone was fit, and the brothers and sisters often moved around the Settlement of Passing with little or no clothing, body consciousness a problem for outsiders. Nakedness was an essential vulnerability, however, for the contests. *Tooth and claw.* Sharpening teeth was forbidden. The nails were to be kept long enough to scratch but too short to pierce. Tooth and claw, the flesh must be torn.

Felix jumped sideways, and a punch probably aimed at his face glanced off his shoulder, spinning him. His feet tangled—*I will not fall on my ass again!*—but he recovered in time for a more successful sidestep of the glancing punch's follow-up.

"HUGE-O! HUGE-O! HUGE-O!"

Swing. Miss. Swing. Miss.

Bludgeoning his opponent into submission was how the revealed True Sons won most contests. Once his rival was slobbering silly and on the edge of unconsciousness, a man could take his time to figure out a way to tear the skin. That was probably why Huge-o focused on using his fists: as big and hard as bricks, they *were* bludgeons. Swing, miss, swing—HIT! Felix thought his right eye socket would collapse into his brain, but he didn't hear or feel bone crack as he again staggered, sideways, backwards, he wasn't sure. Seeing stars, hearing birds chirp, his head was a whirlwind of dizzying clichés. Father watched. Felix's bashed eye closed and wouldn't open, and the other eye only saw, as if through a warped lens, Huge-o growing like the shadow of an eclipse, but Felix could feel Father watching, and he should have felt shame, shame because he was losing in front of Father, but instead—

Father's strength invigorated him. Father expected *him* to be revealed as the True Son. He felt the expectation in his blood. The noon sun blazed overhead. Trees formed a greater circle around the dirt circle where he fought Hugo, who hadn't spent the last six months training to fight, who hadn't overheard a worker from First House say that Father found him "charming." Charm. Charisma. *Essential.* Felix read the books in Father's library. He understood many necessities.

Huge-o grabbed Felix's left shoulder about where the bruise from the glancing punch would be and pulled back his right fist for a blow that might knock Felix's head from his neck. Felix relaxed, became dead weight, and the sudden drop yanked him from Huge-o's grip as he crumpled to the yellow dirt. He rolled, noticing the dirt wasn't all yellow—sun-bleached dried blood from previous contests mixed with the sandy sediment, which contrasted with the grass-covered, deep brown soil surrounding it —and stopped on his back, knees raised to his chest, facing Huge-o's side. The big lug seemed to be having a "Where'd he go?" moment when Felix kicked with both feet into the side of Huge-o's left knee.

POP!

Huge-o yowled, dipped toward Felix, then limped away from him, one, two, three lurching steps. He tried to pivot on his right leg. The thigh and calf of the left leg no longer aligned; the knee was dislocated.

Felix leapt to his feet and in a second stood behind Huge-o, hands clasped together in a double fist, which he swung like a boulder into the right side of Huge-o's head. Huge-o's weight shifted left, and he yowled again as his weight bore down on the crooked leg. He crashed into the dirt. A small cloud rose around him, and whispers rolled through the audience.

Somebody shouted, "Felix!" The crowd did not pick up a chant. Huge-o wasn't out. Lying on his side, he lifted himself with his arms. Father watched. Father wouldn't chant. Father wouldn't cheer. Father wouldn't influence the outcome, at least not in a perceptible way.

From a position in front of him, Felix jumped on Huge-o's cinderblock torso, feet landing on his left side, flattening the bigger man on his back while compressing his ribs.

CRACK!

"OOH!" the audience responded. The audience always responded well to sudden violence, and when one of the contestants ended up prone, like Huge-o was now, excitement became palpable. A few contests ago, Gill, about to be revealed as a True Son, had gotten his adversary on his back and then bitten off his testicles. The shrieks electrified the crowd, who applauded and screamed Gill's name with too much spontaneity to find a rhythm for a chant. Another recent victor, Orion, had stuck his hand inside his opponent's mouth and torn his cheek, then most of his face, off.

One set of broken ribs? Nothing. Felix pounced on Huge-o's

right side.

CRACK!

Huge-o tried to yowl but struggled for breath support. His eyes couldn't have been more open, and his lips quivered. He didn't seem so huge now. He was simply Hugo, and he couldn't sit up. His arms reached in all directions, but they weren't fast or coordinated enough to grab Felix. His size was meaningless. He was meaningless, which was all he could hope for, though now he looked like he hoped for something else.

A girl named Lenora stood at the front of the crowd. Felix didn't know her well, but Hugo talked about her as if she'd been sent from a Heaven nobody believed in. She was pregnant. She shouted, "FELIX!"

Hugo might have heard because his struggles to make noise stopped.

The flesh must be torn.

Felix had no intention of biting off Hugo's balls, and he didn't know how a person actually ripped off another person's face, so he had another plan. He sat on Hugo's left side, sore ass in the dirt, within range of the left arm that flailed along with the right but without much direction. Hugo was like a baby in a crib trying to catch the animals dangling from the mobile high overhead. Drowning in pain and panic, Hugo might have already lost all sense of what was happening. Maybe that was best. Felix grabbed Hugo's left wrist, twisted the arm while pulling it straight and, when it was tense, kicked the back of the elbow.

POP!

Another dislocation. Hugo's body flopped as if on a wave of electricity, and when Felix didn't stop, Hugo's body didn't stop jittering, either. Felix kicked the elbow joint again, pulling on the wrist. Again. Again. The skin stretched. He pulled as hard as he could, and despite his collapsed ribs, Hugo made louder intermittent noises. Felix kept kicking. The bones of the upper arm and forearm separated an inch, two inches. Felix didn't know all the connective tissues he had to break through, but soon only skin held the arm together, so he twisted and pulled, twisted and pulled, twisted and pulled and kicked. The arm broke apart, and red gushed onto the sand.

Father watched.

"Felix! Felix! FELIX!"

The audience needed to be impressed. *Father* needed to be impressed. As quickly as he could manage, using his fingernails and teeth, Felix cleared away gristle, muscle, and skin from the freed bones of the forearm, spitting away anything that got into his mouth without missing a beat. He exposed jagged white that would have to be sharp enough.

Hugo's chest rose and fell in quick, shallow breaths. When he died, the contest would end.

Balancing speed with the slight precision he could muster making long thrusts from above, Felix jammed Hugo's forearm bones into his bare belly, starting below the sternum. Making a jagged line, he stabbed repeatedly until he reached the waist. He set the forearm aside and shoved his fingers into the openings, prying at the edges of individual wounds so the stomach became a single, gaping gash. Reaching in further, feeling the silkiness of inside skin kept safe from air and sun, he pulled out entrails, loops of intestine, the pouch he guessed was the stomach. He stood, carrying the insides with him, and held them up for all to see. Applause roared. Everyone chanted his name.

Father stood from his seat on the dais, and silence was almost immediate. Father set aside his binoculars. "Felix," he said. "My True Son."

Fighting Hugo had made him feel small, but Father addressing him made him feel smaller. In the full sunlight, blood drenched and naked, he held up his friend's entrails like a trophy, and he was absurd. He dropped the guts on the corpse, assuming Hugo was a corpse. At least Hugo wasn't making noise anymore, and he'd bleed to death soon if he hadn't already. For Father, the contest was decided. Father had never addressed Felix directly before, and being the object of Father's attention incapacitated him.

Father, unlike the Father that was, intimidated without

trying. He sat on the high dais that moved from the dirt circle to the amphitheater to First House with pageantry he hadn't jettisoned, but his plain chair was identical to the chairs of the True Sons who decided to join him on the platform, not a gilded throne. The Father that was always wore long robes marked with symbols that had meaning he revealed to the True Sons and no one else, meaning related to abnegation and the void. Father wore simple, loose white pants cinched at the waist, the kind stitched at the Settlement and worn by most men. In warm weather like today's, he went shirtless. The Father that was wore his wild hair and knotted beard long, which made him look older. Father kept his hair short and neat like other men's and was clean shaven, which emphasized his relative youth. No one spoke Father's precise age, but he was too young to be Felix's biological *father*. Nevertheless, he required no ornamentation to be Father.

But no one was beyond ritual. "Ascend the dais," Father commanded.

The crowd around the dirt circle fell away. Felix knew Father and the stairs that led to him. He felt some awareness of the nine other young men on the dais, the other True Sons who had emerged since Father was realized as Father. The True Sons of the Father that was, and the Exalted Brothers who had survived their time as True Sons, were all dead. Nobody knew officially, though everyone knew, how the fire at First House started. It didn't kill anyone, but it flushed the True Sons into the streets and fields of the Nothing Lands, where they limped and stumbled, scratched at their skin and raved about rot. They bled from their eyes, noses, ears, and mouths. They snatched anything sharp they found in workers' hands or anywhere else. They peeled off skin and amputated limbs, screaming about stopping the rot. Some shortened the process by slashing their own throats. Others hacked at themselves until they couldn't anymore. Most of the brothers and sisters witnessed parts of the madness. Witnesses swore that the raving men smelled like rot.

How did Father, the living Father, the True Father, do it?

Felix stood on the dais with him, inches away, looking into

Father's eyes and being looked into. Father put a finger beneath Felix's chin and raised his head higher. "I get a lot of vacant stares around now." Father spoke so only Felix would hear. "I can see the busyness inside your head."

"I'm thinking about you, Father," Felix said.

"What about me?"

Felix cleared his throat and glanced over his shoulder toward the Tree Like All Others. "About the day when you became Father."

"When I tied the old poser to the tree?" Father grinned, still gracing Felix's chin with his touch.

"Yes."

"You must have been... fifteen?"

"Almost sixteen, Father." Sixteen was when a boy gained permission to attend the contests in the dirt circle. When he "tied the old poser to the tree," Father summoned every man, woman, and child in the Lands to witness. Before he said anything about the Father that was, he told everyone to notice the remarkable qualities of the tree to which the man, stripped of his robes, was bound. After a long pause, a girl finally shouted that it looked like all the other trees around it. The man about to be revealed as Father smiled and said she was exactly right. The tree, like the man tied to it, was, in the end, no different from any other. They were nothing.

The younger man removed the older man's head with three swings of an ordinary axe. He only nicked the tree. After that, the younger man was Father. The Father that was, who had established the Nothing Lands decades ago with millions made in industry on the outside, deserved respect, but only Father understood the way forward. Only Father could keep the brothers and sisters moving toward purity.

Father took Felix's bloody right hand into his own clean one. "Do you wish I had secrets to impart, like the meanings the old faker attributed to the scribbles on his costume?" Moving backward, Father drew Felix toward his chair. The nine other True Sons watched. Was being the tenth meaningful or as meaningless as the old Father's symbols, as the Tree Like All Others?

"The ritual is different now," Felix said. "Better."

Without letting go of Felix's hand, Father sat. "Do you seek self-abnegation?"

"Of course." His stomach flipped and knotted because he'd seen eight of the nine True Sons confirmed and so knew what happened next, something he'd done before but never liked, which he knew from school was how things went, different people, different appetites.

Appetite. On the day when he took his place, Father charmed the brothers and sisters with talk about the insignificance of individual trees, individual humans, and the desire for *abnegation*, but they needed more. Ritual. Knowing how to meet people's needs is an aspect of charisma. After the beheading, Father cut out the old faker's heart. And he ate it.

Father said, "On your knees."

Felix knelt in front of him. The audience that had surrounded the dirt circle had crept up to the dais behind him. People murmured. They couldn't see or hear, but they knew. Some called this part Communion. Others called it Joining. Most didn't call it anything.

After today, Felix would live in First House with Father and the other True Sons. During the day, First House stayed open to all brothers and sisters, but what happened there at night, when the doors closed, was private. Would this experience be isolated, or the first of many?

"What happened," Felix muttered.

"What was that?" Father bent forward to listen.

"The axe you killed him with. People say it disappeared." Felix knelt naked between a man's knees, and he was asking about a missing axe.

Father sat back with a laugh. "The tree I tied him to became a holy site. I couldn't stop it. The people insisted on commemorating the damned tree. So, I figured the axe would become a holy object, too. I burned the handle and buried the blade."

A tingling lightness ran from Felix's tailbone to his spine, and he giggled, smiling up at Father in admiration. No bullshit. Father was no bullshit. Felix felt ready.

Father slipped his erect penis out through the flap at the front of his white pants. Relationships were off limits, but boys and girls could play together at night however they wanted as long as they avoided anything that could cause pregnancy, so everybody was always putting everything into everybody else's mouths, and Felix had seen bigger and smaller than what Father offered. Still, having Father's—maybe not holy, but certainly celebrity—dick in his face made him feel at least as exhilarated as he felt queasy. He didn't want to do it, but it was an honor. And if he didn't do it—

Nobody didn't do it.

Probably a death sentence.

A True Son should feel good about sucking his Father's cock.

He took the glans into his mouth and lowered his head into Father's lap.

Sotto voce, the crowd chanted, "*Felix, Felix, Felix!*"

Ignoring the pain from where he'd bitten himself, he kept his lips over his teeth, moved up and down the shaft, and teased the tip with his tongue. The crowd's chant gave him rhythm. Soon, Father's quiet moans gave him inspiration. Father was pleased.

When Father came in his mouth, ejaculating into the back of his throat, he almost choked.

2. THE POPULATION

"I'm not ready! Not like this! Please!" The woman full of protests looked young, maybe close to Felix's age, which would make this one her first. She had the bed closest to the small one-room medical building's main door. The woman on the other bed looked older, maybe mid-twenties, and much calmer. She'd probably been through this procedure once, maybe even twice, before. Women only had to survive three times to fulfill their obligations.

Death required living.

Marianne came back into the building wearing scrubs, surgical gloves, a surgical mask, a soft cap over her pinned-up silver hair, and what looked like safety glasses. She checked the readouts on the monitors for the two women's vitals. "You, missy, need to calm down."

"PLEASE!"

"Shush. It'll all be decided soon." Marianne sounded like grandmothers were supposed to sound, cheery and indulgent, though nobody who grew up in the Lands knew anything about their grandparents or parents. Some kids who came in as toddlers claimed to have memories that gave them suspicions about who their parents might be, but they were never sure.

"Please, if you loosen the restraints—"

Marianne belly laughed. Her belly was bigger than most. Felix guessed she was in her sixties, which made her one of the oldest people in the Settlement of Passing, certainly the oldest woman. On the outside, she'd been a nurse, and the Father that was had recruited her directly from a suicide support group. Why she chose to keep living and perform her current functions mystified Felix, but the Father that was had regarded her as a pillar of the community, and Father did the same. Even the True Sons deferred to her. Father was life and death, but so, in a way, was she.

"You seem like you've got yourself under control," Marianne said to the quieter woman who was not struggling against the leather restraints that bound her to the flat medical bed. She'd also been perfectly calm while Marianne had cleaned and disinfected her. "You're Beth, right?"

"I'm surprised you remember me."

"Last time you weren't as easy-breezy." Marianne brushed a lock of black hair away from Beth's face. "Maybe you could help me explain to the new girl—"

"Darlene, my name's Darlene!" Darlene's hair was light brown and had waves in it distorted by tangles and frizz. Her pale skin glowed. Not panicked and restrained, she might have been pretty.

"Maybe you could help me explain to Darlene that there's only foolishness in loosening the restraints, because if she slipped away, what would she do? Run away from the Lands? Have that baby on the outside? Make two foxes for the hunt?"

"You don't want to be hunted, Darlene," Beth said.

"Take a good look at her, Felix." Marianne belly laughed again. Felix stepped closer, happy to be acknowledged for the first time. "Little Miss Foxy here could be your first hunt. The Sons caught the last one before she even went into labor, brought her back in rough shape, but she lived. Had the baby in confinement. But the baby wasn't welcome back home any more than she was."

"Wha… what happened to the…" For some reason, Darlene turned her head toward Felix. He felt self-conscious looking at the naked woman with the enormous belly drenched in panic sweat from head to foot.

"You've lived your whole life here," Marianne said. She didn't need specific knowledge of Darlene to make such a claim: no child over three was ever admitted into the Nothing Lands, so if a young woman was around Felix's age and nine months pregnant, she grew up here. Felix didn't know her, but boys and girls didn't mix in school, and nighttime frolics were often anonymous. Marianne continued, "You've never known hunger or thirst. They can make you do things you'd never dream of doing normally."

Felix got her meaning. Darlene did, too, judging from her pallor.

"Things got worse for her. Things can always get worse." Marianne looked at the small table with her metal tray of nightmarish tools, refined cutting implements, blades of different lengths and curvatures. A large saw looked out of place. It had a squatty U-shaped chrome handle too big for the tray and a straight shiny blade with many small teeth.

"I don't want to die." Darlene punctuated the outrageous statement with an obnoxious snort.

"Nonsense!" Marianne tsk-tsked. "What foolishness has gotten into your head? What about *you*, Beth? Do you want to die?"

"Yes," Beth said. "I haven't reached a point in my journey where I am certain about *when* and *how*, but if I go today..." she shrugged as much as the restraints would allow, "meh."

"It's exciting," Marianne said. "Your third. Are you hoping for a girl?"

Death required living. A girl meant survival.

"If it would please Father," Beth said. "Father is life and death."

"Yes, dear, so he is." Marianne pressed a firm hand on Darlene's forehead, thwarting in advance the attempt to struggle as Marianne looped the final restraint around Darlene's neck.

Darlene closed her eyes. "Please, Father, let it be a girl."

Father discouraged people from praying to him, as he did not claim divinity, but people prayed to him anyway. What a thing, to be prayed to. Quite a thing. Darlene desired Father's blessing without irony or resentment. She knew Father's rules spelled out her predicament. Felix had questioned the apparent arbitrariness of ritual. Had she? During a trip outside, Salvador, Father's first True Son, had told him that the brutality was not arbitrary. A calculus of suffering informed the confrontation with the void; the Land's traditions and rituals all enhanced the confrontation.

Marianne picked up a scalpel.

Felix glanced at the monitors as beeping signaled another escalation of Darlene's heart rate. She whined, a sound from the back of her throat, and her lips stretched in a wide, quivering oval. Marianne lifted her scalpel and examined the blade, which glinted in the light from the conical fixture dangling overhead.

Why, if we're focused on death, do we devote such time and effort to babies, the nursery, school… what's the point of reproduction at all?

Salvador ruffled his hair. "We're not all drinking poisoned Kool-Aid or hoping to ride en masse on a spaceship hiding behind a comet. Everybody dies alone. We are a web of solitary travelers seeking death in our own ways. We cannot search for death without life. Death requires living."

Father's wisdom, Salvador's puffy-lipped mouth that made women swoon.

The ritual, the calculus of suffering, surrounding childbirth didn't call for a large audience like the making of a True Son, but it did require a True Son as witness, the role Felix was performing for his first time. The Settlement could have afforded an ultrasound machine to track fetal development and determine sex in advance, but it didn't have one, and Felix reasoned it didn't because finding out the baby's sex and its consequences was part of the ritual. Likewise, the medical facility could have provided anesthesia—which was available for other procedures—but it did not.

Darlene screamed as Marianne cut into her lower abdomen, splitting open skin with a transverse incision about four inches wide. The incision spread as if the skin felt relieved from being stretched over the belly bulge. Marianne, slow and steady despite Darlene's howls, used a clean white towel to pat away blood that spilled into the opening. The cutting continued past the outer, surprisingly thin layer of skin into some yellowish stuff, followed by red cords, probably muscle, which Marianne pushed past.

Beneath she cut into thicker yellow-white spongy material, Felix guessed fat, and with short slices, the blade deepened the incision. Darlene's initial scream turned into an ongoing noise of terror and pain, syncopated by the rhythm of Marianne's cuts.

"You think Mama's going to pass out?" Marianne yelled to be heard over Darlene's noise, and Felix took a moment to realize that she was yelling at him. "Here." She set the bloody towel on Darlene's belly and grabbed an instrument resembling a small, bent spade. "Use this to hold the bottom of the incision open for me."

Felix studied the instrument for a moment, figured out how the curved part could hook the loose lower lip of the wound, put it in place, and pulled the incision wider so that Marianne could see her own cutting. He also took the bloody towel and cleared away gathering fluid.

"Thank you," the former nurse said. "After the fat, what you see here is the peritoneal wall," reddish-pink, not as vibrant as the muscles, "which we cut, and… there's the uterus!" Gray and shiny, trying to pop out—"And we cut…." Viscous fluid burst and splashed on Felix's hands, and Felix saw a small coil of purplish-blue umbilical rope.

Darlene's noise became coherent. "Don't want to, don't want, don't," she sobbed.

Marianne set aside the scalpel and reached through the mess, into the opening, and gripped what was inside. Felix stepped back as she pulled out the baby headfirst but flipped it upside down while turning to block Darlene's view. She looked like she was kissing it, then spat. She patted its back and cleaned out its mouth with her finger. A few seconds later, it cried.

He cried.

Marianne cut the cord, swaddled the baby, and set him in one of the wicker bassinets prepared with a warming pad and many blankets.

Fighting for breath, Darlene asked, "What is it?" Somehow, she'd stayed conscious through the pain. Somehow, she remained concerned about what happened next.

"Congratulations," Marianne said.

Felix looked into Darlene's eyes. She did look familiar. Of course she did. They'd grown up together. His mind was a blank now, but later, he'd remember her. An image would come into his mind other than what he'd seen today. Other than what he was about to see.

"Do me a favor, Felix, and hand me another towel." Marianne's white gloves had turned red.

"Sure." Felix fetched a towel from the pile next to the tray of implements. His eyes caught Darlene's again, and something she saw jolted her.

"No!" she yelled. "NO!"

Felix tried not to look at her again as he handed Marianne the towel. Marianne didn't bother wiping off her gloved hands. She shoved the towel in Darlene's mouth. Darlene made noises behind the gag.

Marianne retrieved the scalpel. Felix knew what came next from his own childhood and because, like everyone else, he'd studied the process for legitimate births in the Lands at school. He'd also studied natural births and knew that at this point, C-section or otherwise, the afterbirth usually made an exit, but now it wouldn't. Instead, Marianne went back to cutting. She started at each corner of the gaping wound. The scalpel slit skin, which wasn't as eager as before to spread but nevertheless pulled apart as the blade moved from side to side, widening the opening. Blood dripping into hair made Felix more aware of how close the incision got to Darlene's pubic area, the vulva, labial folds, and he felt self-conscious again as Marianne extended the split in Darlene's skin all the way to her hips.

Trading the scalpel for curved scissors, Marianne didn't move around muscle this time. She cut through. Darlene whimpered beneath the gag. Her eyelids fluttered. Felix got another towel to sop up blood near where Marianne worked, but the bleeding became heavier and heavier. Sight wasn't much of an option. Marianne had to be feeling her way through as she dug into the spongy layer of yellow-white fat.

Somehow, she widened access to the peritoneum without damaging what was beneath.

Every boy growing up in the Nothing Lands lived in the nursery dorms until age twelve, and a glass case built into the wall above his bunk displayed something he usually didn't learn about until he was six or seven years old. The cases displayed what generally looked like similarly shaped lumps of meat, different shades of pink and red, a big central mass, two nubby arms and a tail-like extension. They were mysteries for the little kids, and the big kids didn't tell because they'd get in trouble. Rumors got around, though, and kids said it had something to do with your *parents*. Some said it had to do with your *mother*. Girls didn't have them, only boys. These hints made the curiosity more and more titillating.

Finally, during a conference, a nice young teacher, Nicholas, told Felix he would never know who his mother was or anything else about her, but the meat on display over his bunk was her womb, along with her ovaries and cervix and other things that didn't matter. The womb was the place where she had carried him for nine months so that he could be born into the world and begin his journey toward death. It was like the stars in the sky or Father's words, miraculous and transcendent and his in a way nothing else but death would ever be. *His.*

At age six, Felix learned the word "transcendent" and held onto it.

He watched Marianne rip the transcendent womb from Darlene's dying body. Darlene had lost consciousness at some point. When didn't matter.

Marianne held up the uterus, fallopian tubes, ovaries, and cervix attached, and said, "Got to get this to the Preservationist." After setting the organs by the occupied bassinet, she pressed a button on the wall. Felix heard a faint buzz.

He jumped at Beth's soft voice: "What do you think so far?"

Darlene's open abdomen, the blood-drenched sheets and mattress beneath her, the growing puddles on the tile floor, the exception to her motionlessness, small spasms in her chest that must have been breaths. Hugo might have been dead when Felix had reached in and brought his insides out. Darlene had certainly been alive when Marianne had torn out her woman parts. She might live longer.

Felix looked at Beth. "I think it's harder to watch than to learn about in school," he said. Beth didn't have the same potential to be pretty that Darlene had, or once had, but she had warm brown eyes like two cookies and an endearing softness of expression. He didn't need to see a repeat performance. Beth having a girl would be okay with him.

"What about the next step in the ritual?" Beth asked.

Felix tried to swallow. Failing, he said, "You mean your turn?"

"No. What happens to her."

Small spasms in Darlene's chest. He knew what happened months after she died, but now? No clue.

Two men entered through the main door. One took the occupied bassinet, the other the evacuated womb. They exited in opposite directions. Marianne closed the door behind them and returned to Darlene's bedside.

"I don't know what happens to her... now." Felix looked at Marianne and blushed, uncertain whether he should be talking to Beth.

Marianne belly laughed. "What happens now is a lot different than it used to be, but I guess you wouldn't know that, Beth, because you're still young. I've got to do what I've got to do because the butcher got old and lazy and comfortable and had what he called a 'renegotiation' that stuck even when the Father that was became a was, and Father was revealed."

Felix had no idea what she was talking about. Beth stared at the ceiling. Her monitor revealed growing anxiety. Darlene's monitor revealed almost nothing.

Marianne picked up the saw with the squatty U-shaped handle that overlapped the edges of the tray of cutting implements.

"She's too far gone to scream," Beth said, "and I don't have to watch this part again." Face to the ceiling, she closed her eyes. "Felix, you're the witness."

Marianne held the saw in one hand and a bloody towel in the other. "It's not so bad, Felix, but I *do* want the butcher to finish his journey so I can give back this part of the job to whatever young man takes his place. Anyway, check this out." She tossed the blood-thickened towel into the air and swiped at it with the saw, which halved the heavy fabric like tissue paper. "No electric saw on the market is half as sharp."

Felix looked at the incision in Darlene's abdomen, once a few inches, now a fissure as wide as her hips. Small spasms in her chest. Smaller and smaller.

"No time like the present," Marianne said. "We start with the wings." She picked up one of Darlene's arms, positioned the saw at the top of the shoulder, and moved the blade slowly back and forth, forming a groove beneath the rotator cuff. Darlene didn't react. With the groove established, she made faster, heavier movements back and forth, driving the blade downward through the arm in a spurt of red. Three back-and-forth slides of the blade through the groove were all Marianne needed to disconnect the arm almost completely. It dangled from stubborn gristle. Much as Felix had with Hugo's elbow, Marianne pulled the arm away from its former point of attachment. She'd called the arm a "wing." It was like pulling off the wing of a roasted turkey at a feast. With a swipe of the long blade, Marianne broke the wing free.

Felix expected her to remove the other arm, but she bore down the saw next to the neck instead. Blood leaked, but it didn't spurt. No more little spasms. Darlene was dead, but her death was incidental. Marianne cut along the spine almost halfway down, then back up above the ribs to the shoulder blade. "Chuck," she said.

Who was Chuck?

Marianne cut along the spine again, then cut outward to the sides until she could slide out half of Darlene's ribs in a block. "I *don't* have to remove the organs, and I *don't* have to get the meat off the bones."

A diagram he'd seen somewhere—not in the Lands because they didn't eat red meat—flashed in his mind. A cow, in profile, had its body divided into sections named for different types of meat. Such as ribs. Such as chuck. The last time he checked, cows didn't have wings... but Marianne was allowed to mix meat metaphors. The butcher would get his meat pre-butchered. Marianne, soaked in dead Darlene's persistent wet, should have been above this kind of work, but he'd renegotiated.

The venerable lady sawed off Darlene's calves beneath the knees and thighs beneath the hips. The body from beneath the ribs to the pelvis remained intact, withered testimony to the purpose she had served. Again, Marianne only needed three back-and-forth movements of the saw blade in a groove to remove Darlene's head, starting beneath the chin. The chest, tits included, was a single piece. Finished, Marianne said, "That ought to be compact enough. What do you think?"

Dazed and bleary, Felix nodded.

Marianne retrieved a cardboard box with a silvery internal lining and arranged Darlene's parts inside. She sealed the box with packing tape and turned to Felix. "Would you be a hero and help me carry this over to the door?"

Felix agreed as his mind filled with the rest of the process. The butcher still had far more work to do because he *did* have to remove the organs and get the meat off the bones. All the meat had to be collected and reduced—chopped small and ground and minced and pureed—so that it had a consistent, ultra-soft texture. Somewhere along the line it would be cooked, but the important thing was that it be preserved, not like the womb, which was preserved like a trophy for years and years of evolving appreciation. Mother's meat had to wait for baby to be ready for solid food. Six months or so.

Every boy had to eat his mother. That's what they taught in school. After a boy left the nursery for the adolescent dorms, he learned that for years he'd been staring not only at the womb in which he'd been carried but at the only fleshy part of his mother he hadn't consumed. The womb-burning that followed was part of the ascension to a new phase of living and another stride taken toward the end. The idea that any part of life was inherently nurturing had to be given up to achieve adulthood.

They set the box by the door, and Marianne pressed the button on the wall. Minutes later, men came and took away the box. Marianne crossed to the sink on one side of the room, stripped her gloves, and scrubbed her hands. As she got herself new gloves, she said, "You scrub in, too. And wear gloves this time. You're helpful."

Felix mimicked the way he'd seen Marianne wash her hands, and he didn't comment on how strange the latex gloves felt against his skin.

They stood on either side of Beth's bed. "Hon, there's no point in holding back from screaming. It hurts like the dickens, and there's no prize for denying it."

When Marianne started the incision in Beth's lower abdomen, Felix mopped blood with a towel, more aware of Beth's nakedness and the closeness of her genitals but less self-conscious. Beth cried out, but the sound was more like a loud dissolve into tears than an actual scream. He admired Beth. He hoped for a girl. How did women not hate all men when maleness was so catastrophic?

Because Father was a man. Father was father of all. The only parent any of them knew.

Father was life *and* death. Hating death meant hating Father. Death required living. Living required death.

Hating death was insanity.

Through the skin, around the muscle, through the fat, through the peritoneum, into the uterus, a gush of fluid, Marianne reached in, retrieved the newborn, held it upside down, shielded it from the mother's view, and, after she cleared its airways, she helped it cry.

Felix lit up, and despite the tears of agony rolling down her cheeks, Beth smiled at him.

"You spoiler, you!" Marianne admonished. She'd seen what had passed between him and Beth. The new confidence he'd found fled. He blushed, knowing his face must be beet-red. "Well, to make it official, congratulations, hon, on having your third girl. Now you can get old and gray like me, if that's where your journey takes you."

Marianne cut the cord, swaddled the baby girl, delivered her to a bassinet, and pressed a button. She hurried back to Beth, who moaned but seemed delirious enough to be missing out on most of the pain. "Now I've got to get the rest out of you," she said, reaching into the incision, "and stitch you up before you lose too much—wait a minute."

The sudden seriousness on Marianne's face stunned Felix more than her words. What could go wrong now?

"There's somebody else in here."

When women scheduled to conceive went to the fertilization rooms, they had at least four or five men in a night. Biological fathers weren't known—Father was father of all—so predicting the possibility, or probability, of twins—

"NO!" Beth screamed.

The heart rate monitor beeped erratically. Beth must have felt what he felt in his gut. They wouldn't be identical twins. They'd be fraternal. After three, her luck had run out. This fourth baby would be a boy.

"Felix, I need you to turn around," Marianne said.

"What?"

Beth screamed.

"TURN AROUND! DON'T LOOK!"

Felix turned around.

Beth became quiet. Marianne was quiet. Felix resisted the urge to look over his shoulder.

After a while, Felix heard a quiet sob. Beth. "It's okay," Marianne said.

"W-what?" Beth's question betrayed no iota of belief.

"Felix, come see for yourself. He's dead." In her hands, Marianne held a still infant boy with bluish skin smudged by red and flecks of the unknown. "He must have suffocated before I got to him."

While Felix considered the situation, Marianne set the dead baby on the abandoned bloody bed, removed the afterbirth, and worked on sewing Beth back together. "If there's no baby boy," he said, "there's no need to complete the ritual."

"True." Marianne did not look up from her work.

Should one congratulate a mother on the death of her child? "You'll be okay, Beth," he said.

"Fucking hell," Beth said.

Marianne disposed of the dead infant and the afterbirth in the same bin.

3. PRACTICE

No taller than five and a half feet, sixteen-year-old Jordan looked ridiculous with the oblong black bag strapped to his back. It stuck up high enough to provide a headrest and bounced against his butt while he walked. His black pants kept the butt-bouncing from being too awfully noticeable, but it still looked silly. They needed to avoid drawing attention, especially because Jordan had dark skin, and people with dark skin were more likely to be searched or, worse, shot by authorities. If asked about the bag, they had a ready explanation—it held Jordan's oboe; they were on a school trip to play a concert in the prestigious Mansworth Music Center—but Felix couldn't allow a search, and he couldn't allow either of them to be apprehended.

Jordan's ears looked scared. Felix could understand seeing fear in a person's eyes and mouth, but fear in the ears was new. When the boy spoke, he kept his voice steady, but he didn't seem capable of much volume, which made hearing difficult as traffic growled along the streets by the sidewalks they traveled. Though he might have shared Felix's concerns about avoiding nosy authorities, Jordan was more likely afraid of, well, everything. The world. The people of the Nothing Lands liked staying apart, but the Lands weren't a prison. Barring pregnancy, adults could come and go at will. Starting at age sixteen, kids could leave with adult supervision, but before that, for safety, kids stayed in the Settlement. The Settlement, however, didn't exist in a vacuum. In school, children studied news from the outside. They got to know its terrors, its bleakness, its chaos. Such study instilled appreciation for a ritualized, regimented life that combined death not with ubiquitous decay but with devotion and dignity.

Jordan and Felix stopped at a crosswalk where the light flashed "DON'T WALK." Crosswalks, traffic lights, buildings tall enough to block out the sun, awnings, shops, street vendors, drivers, pedestrians, people, people, and more people: Jordan had surely seen the overwhelming massiveness on television, in movies, and in video games, but the sublimity of the in-person encounter must have been keeping his head and eyes in constant motion as he tried to ingest the reality of it all. "How much farther?" the boy asked.

Felix looked at the cell phone, which was using an app with GPS to show their position on a city map, amusing technology that had no use in the Lands and wouldn't work there anyway. "A couple of blocks until we get to his building. A block is the distance between—"

"I know what a block is," Jordan said, too testily for Felix's liking.

"You know why we make sacrifices?" Felix looked down at his young companion. Passersby on the crowded sidewalk were invisible.

Jordan couldn't have sounded more mechanical: "To demonstrate and celebrate the beauty of death."

"You know why I brought you here?"

"Practice," Jordan said.

Felix bumped into a woman wearing a top with the front cut so low that it almost showed nipples. He saw only cleavage and said, "Excuse me."

"Fuck off, jerk." She moved along, and he never saw her face.

Resuming his pace with Jordan, Felix said, "Why do you practice?"

"Because practice makes perfect?" Jordan grinned.

"You know I'll report back to your teachers," Felix said.

Jordan traded the grin for a return to the mechanistic. "Because if Father is pleased to call on me for a sacrifice, I must be prepared to impress him."

"How do you impress him?"

"With HIM."

"What is HIM?"

"Heartiness, Innovation, and...." Jordan lowered his head and giggled.

Felix giggled, too, then joined his answer in unison, using exaggerated tones: "And *MOXIE!*"

They laughed together, and Felix felt glad to see Jordan relax as they approached the high-rise apartment building the app marked as their destination. A short flight of stairs led up to the front door, which required a key card for entry. "What now?" Jordan asked.

"Now, we wait. Look *nonchalant*."

"Nonchalant?" Jordan giggled.

Felix laughed. "None shall aunt."

A shadowy corner by the stairs would probably be inconspicuous enough for waiting but not too far away. Felix took the pack of cigarettes from his pocket. Nobody in the Lands smoked, but a cigarette made a good prop at a time like this. He lit up.

"So, can you tell me now?" Jordan asked.

"Tell you what?" Felix sucked smoke into his mouth but blew it out without inhaling. The things people did to their bodies were disgusting.

"This guy, what was his name, Angus?"

"Gus Merriweather."

"Well, you worked on the prelims. What can you tell me about him?"

Felix considered. "He's forty-three."

"Whoa," Jordan said. Forty-three was old by the Lands' standards, not here outside.

"Skin like mine, dusty hair, bald on top."

"I guess I'll see him soon enough," Jordan said. "But what makes him... why does he deserve it?"

"Everyone deserves it. You do. I do. He does."

"Okay, yeah, I know," Jordan said, "but we've walked by, like, thousands of people to get to this one guy."

Felix shrugged. "What can I say? Gus is a nice guy."

"He's a sacrifice—no, not as good as that—a *practice* sacrifice because he's a nice guy?" Jordan reached for Felix's cigarette, which Felix handed over. He took a drag and seemed to hold his breath as he passed the smoking stick back. A second later, he coughed and kept coughing.

Over the coughs, Felix said, "There's no better reason than being a nice guy. A few years ago, or whatever, he was close to suicide because his wife died. Some sickness nobody in the Lands would ever get. Instead of killing himself, though, he rebounded. Started donating half his considerable income to charities. Do you know what a soup kitchen is?"

Jordan went for the mechanical: "A shoddy attempt to address the ravages of income inequality by—"

"Okay, fine. Mr. Merriweather works in one three nights a week." Felix sucked smoke into his mouth and blew it out. "Mr. Merriweather is an enemy of despair, which would make his death a poignant demonstration."

"If it wasn't just for practice," Jordan said.

"Call it a poignant lesson," Felix said.

"Wouldn't you think that something reflecting the arbitrariness of—"

"Shh!" Felix pointed at the building's front door, stomped out his cigarette, and led Jordan to the front step as two women exited the building. "You'll never believe what Gus has done with the place!" Felix said, climbing quickly.

"I should have ordered an Uber," one woman said to the other. They both looked older—fifties? "Or do you think we'll be able to walk half a block and get a cab right away?" How much did old people think about being old?

The women didn't hurry down the steps, and the door was closing behind them. If Felix pushed them out of the way, he might arouse suspicion, so he passed at their rate, stepped around them, and shoved his foot into the doorway as it was about to snap shut. The women didn't look back as he swung the door wide, passing the knob to Jordan.

Like the building itself, the lobby was narrow, big enough for the stairwell, a waiting area for the elevator, and a desk for a thirty-ish man in a red vest and white shirt. Felix assumed he was a building attendant. The man stood, his chair rolling away behind him. "What can I do for you young gentlemen?"

With a hand on Jordan's shoulder to keep him moving, Felix headed for the stairs. "Going up to see Gus." Felix only gave the attendant a glance.

"Hold on a minute," the red-vested man said. "You mean Gus Merriweather? Come see me over here for a minute, please."

Nonchalant. They would be nonchalant. They reversed down the few stairs they had climbed, and Felix led toward the desk. "Yeah, Gus, on the fourth floor. He didn't go into the lab today."

Felix and Jordan faced the attendant across the desk. "Is he expecting you?"

With a huff, Felix said, "He'd better be. Dad made the arrangements."

"I'll give him a call to say you're on your way up." The attendant reached for the phone on his desk.

Shit. Shit, shit, shit. "It's okay," Felix said. "His phone's on mute, but I texted him from outside." Felix unshouldered his own, regularly shaped backpack and set it on the desk's edge. "Let me show you my phone." He unzipped the bag's main compartment.

"Wait—what—your phone's in your backpack?" The attendant looked conflicted. "And you—your bag... what are you carrying? You maybe should both—"

"Oboe," Jordan said, the fear in his voice as audible as the word he articulated. "Concert."

Felix's backpack had rope and duct tape, always field necessities, as well as the roll of thin wire and box of needles Jordan had requested. Beneath the drill and the stud finder's plastic bulk, Felix found the folded knife and opened its serrated three-inch blade while it was still hidden in the bag.

The attendant leaned over to look in the bag. "Can't find your phone?"

The reduced distance between them allowed Felix to do what was necessary in two movements: he pulled his arm, knife in hand, out of the bag, and he jammed the knife into the attendant's throat. The attendant stood up straight behind the desk, staggered back, and groped at the handle protruding from his neck. He couldn't scream or call for help. Blood streamed from the sides of the puncture and rose to his mouth, which half-puckered like a fish's as red spilled over his bottom lip. Felix walked around to the attendant's side of the desk, grabbed the knife handle, and jerked it to one side, severing the jugular as he pushed the attendant to his knees and tipped him to the floor.

The desk would hide the body, but not for very long. "Let's get this done," Felix said. He wiped the knife and his hand on the attendant's clothes and reshouldered his pack.

Jordan nodded. They raced up the stairs to the fourth floor.

Felix got them to the apartment's front door, but from that point, Jordan had to lead. The building's front door had a modern entry system, but the apartment doors had regular locks for regular keys, which school had taught Jordan to handle. Jordan took off his bag—time to get all the tools ready anyway—and unzipped it.

A trained eye probably would have identified Jordan's bag as one made for rifles, not oboes, but the rifle inside wasn't made for killing. It shot darts, tranquilizer darts by design, though it carried different ammunition today. Jordan didn't take out the rifle yet. He unzipped one of the rifle bag's outer pouches and retrieved the small vinyl kit, which, when also unzipped, revealed a variety of thin metal tools, some of them two-pronged, some of them jagged, some of them smooth.

Jordan knelt in front of Mr. Merriweather's door, which had two locks. The top was round and looked like a bolt. The bottom was built into the door handle. Jordan selected his tools. "What if he hears the locks jiggle?"

"He might open the door," Felix said. "Would you be ready?"

Jordan's pleading expression seemed to say, *Aren't we in this together now?* Then he said, "No," and took the dart rifle out of the bag.

"Good," Felix said.

"What if he calls the police? What if someone sees the body downstairs and calls the police?"

Felix sighed, unzipped the rifle bag's other small pouch, and readied his handgun. "We improvise."

"Improvise." Jordan leaned the rifle against the wall and got to work on the locks, turning each in under a minute, which was better than Felix could have done, but that information wasn't to be shared. "You know, I didn't think to check the hall for security cameras."

"And if I were actually scoring you, you would have lost points for that, but don't worry," Felix said. "I've been pretty thorough, and I haven't seen a camera in the building, which is something we look for in the prelims anyway."

Jordan put away his lockpick set, put the empty bag on his back, held the rifle in one hand, and gripped the doorknob with the other. With half a voice, he said, "Time to go in."

"After you, sir."

Jordan turned the knob and pushed the door inward with slowness that only exaggerated the hinges' creak, but unless the situation got out of hand, Jordan would make all his own choices now. The practice sacrifice was an initiation, one of their most important rituals of passage, and each child of the Lands had one opportunity, no matter how it turned out. Captured and killed were identical outcomes, Father would ensure. The practice sacrifice provided many kids' first intimate experiences in proximity with death, their own and another's. In the moment, fear blocked out finer sensation, but for Felix, like for most others, the experience later became a source of exhilaration recollected in tranquility.

Crouching, dart rifle in both hands, Jordan led into the broad entryway, which had an open door into the bathroom on the left and a sink by the smallest microwave/stove/oven combo Felix had ever seen, which, all combined with some cabinets and a small fridge, were probably supposed to be the kitchen section of what people would likely describe as a "studio" apartment. The rest looked like a bedroom, though a loveseat and coffee table did sit by the bed facing the direction of the wall-mounted television. On the far side of the room, next to the big window, was a desk with an enormous computer monitor. At the desk, on a chair with wheels that looked like it would swivel, sat a man with fair skin and dusty hair that didn't quite cover his head. He wore headphones, though. Headphones, a t-shirt, and boxer shorts.

On the big computer screen, colors and shapes linked at points labeled by alphanumeric abbreviations. Felix recognized the type of diagram as a chemical structure, but he couldn't make sense of it. No time anyway, but he remembered Salvador calling this man *Doctor* Angus Merriweather. Felix wondered about the selection process for practice sacrifices, or all sacrifices.

The Father that was had been a doctor. MD/PhD. His millions had come from pharmaceutical patents. In the Lands, he continued his work and had a private "grow house" attached to First House. Mostly mushrooms, people said. Only the Father to be revealed worked with him there, like only Salvador worked with Father there now. Felix hoped to be admitted. He did very well in Chemistry, and he never stopped studying.

Jordan aimed at Gus's upper back, the portion not blocked by the chair. "Remember," Felix said. "No more than three shots." Jordan nodded, squinted, and squeezed the trigger. With a *piw!*, the dart flew into the t-shirt and made a small red circle. First, Gus kept looking at the screen, and absent-minded fingers scratched at the dart. When they collided with the protuberance, they froze. He pulled off his headphones—bass thumped—and swiveled.

"WHO THE HELL—" He got to his feet.

Piw! Piw!

Both darts hit his chest, and the hand that had scratched at the first offender slapped at them like mosquitoes, and he cried out when he drove the sharp points deeper into his skin. "What the...?!"

"He didn't go down," Jordan mumbled.

"It takes a few seconds."

Slurring, Gus said, "Who are you? What did you do to me?" He stepped forward, then lunged at the rifle.

Jordan yelped and tried to yank the gun away. Gus grabbed the barrel.

"Don't shoot!" Felix commanded. He shouldn't have tried to help.

A tug of war ensued, during which Gus became rubberier and rubberier. He pulled on the gun; Jordan pulled back, almost lifting the larger man from his feet. Gus found steadiness and pulled. Jordan again almost lifted him. Gus pulled, let go, and fell. On his back, he looked around him, eyes wild. "Where the hell am I?" he asked, slurring more than before. "How did I—" He stopped moving.

Salvador explained that the darts contained a drug similar to rocuronium or succinylcholine, a paralytic that would keep the target from being able to move a muscle while still feeling and perceiving, perhaps through some confusion, all that occurred.

"Is it time?" Jordan asked.

"You tell me," Felix said. He looked at the big digital clock by the bed. The drug would last an hour, give or take, so that wasn't a problem. They'd been sloppy with the building attendant. A pool of blood might spread out under the desk, into the main walkway between the stairs and the elevator. Anybody going in or out might—

"Give me your bag," Jordan said.

Que sera, sera. Felix handed over the backpack, sat in the desk chair, and rolled as far out of the way as he could get while Jordan went to work.

The boy used the coffee table for a boost but still had to stand on his tiptoes to feel around the ceiling with the stud finder. With appropriate places located at a good distance from each other, Jordan started holes with the drill and then screwed in the eye bolts the rest of the way. He ran rope through one loop and, after fumbling with Gus as if he were the world's largest sack of potatoes, tied a tight circle around Gus's wrist. Then he had a pulley for lifting Gus's wrist, the rest of him attached, toward the ceiling.

"Shit," Jordan said. "Forgot." He cut the shirt around Gus's lifted arm and fought to get the rest over parts still free. Removing the shorts was easier. He tied up the naked man's other wrist and lifted it to the ceiling. Gus's suspended hands stretched far enough from each other to make the skin between the shoulders taut, but his chest and belly still sagged, flabby with age and overeating.

Felix wished Gus could talk. His thoughts at this moment must have been fascinating.

Jordan found the other knife in Felix's backpack, the skinning knife with the curved blade and the hooked tip. As soon as he had it, he sliced from the side of the left arm to the shoulder, under the collar bone, to the next shoulder, along the right arm, and stopped at the right wrist. Stretched skin peeked open, bleeding in spaced droplets like rain from a cracked window. Jordan picked up speed, started at the center of the collar bone, and sliced downward as if unzipping the chest and stomach, cutting a vertical line to form a T with his first horizontal cut. Crouching, he cut a from left hip rightward, under the navel, to the right hip, and Felix thought of Darlene and wondered if Jordan had something planned for Gus's guts. He had a better sense, though, because the skin of Gus's torso had become a sideways H, a set of double doors, and Jordan had wanted a skinning knife so he could open him up.

The knife was sharp, so Jordan could separate the skin from the body with ease, pulling at the epidermis on top and making gentle chops at the membranous connective tissues underneath that didn't want to let go. A few sloppy cuts broke blood vessels, which led to some gushes, but Jordan aimed to keep the skin thin and intact, peeling off in sheets, so the blood leaked but didn't pour. Every inch Jordan peeled away, of course, was attached to the nerves underneath, so, while paralyzed and unable to move the muscles that Jordan was exposing to light, Gus felt every movement of his skin away from his body, every chop, every pull, every tear. He felt his torso opening, each revelatory tug. His head dangled, pointing his eyes downward. He *saw* his torso opening.

Near the bottom of the open torso, Felix recognized spongy yellow-white fat. A similar substance appeared throughout the exposed area, in blobs and loose clusters, along with muscles like in diagrams and veiny-artery-looking things that squiggled around and in and out like worms. What wasn't like the diagrams was how *gelatinous* it all looked. Gus was gooey. This was the Adventure of Gooey Gus.

Jordan took the wire and needles from the backpack and sewed the corners of Gus's torso doorway to the eye bolts so that the wires held the doors open. He repeated the process with Gus's back, cutting the sideways H, cutting between skin and muscle, opening the doors, and tying them to the eye bolts. Gus Merriweather became an exhibit *in the round*.

Bare arms and bare thighs gave up flaps of skin to be held open in the web of thin wire before Jordan finally said, "Okay! Done!" He was covered in blood. Jordan hadn't requested a change of clothes, so they hadn't brought one for him. An allowed oversight. Now wasn't the time to alert him to the problem. He looked proud.

"Fine work," Felix said. Done in thirty minutes. "Good cutting technique. Nice visual display." He could have shown more *moxie*. Flaying was too common. Felix thought Jordan might have tried something with the muscles underneath, some reordering of them, knotting up their strips like balloon animals. He'd bring up the need for creativity in a later review. Now, the boy could have his pride.

His face betrayed something behind the pride. Wooziness, maybe. "Thank you," he said, but he wasn't all there.

"Is Gus alive?"

Jordan studied Gus until movement revealed breath. "Yes. Yes!" Jordan beamed. "I did it all without killing him."

"Should we leave him like that?"

"No. I guess not," Jordan said.

"But we should be going?"

"There's still the body downstairs to think about. I should have done something about that." Jordan's beam dimmed. "We should get out of here, fast."

"Probably." Felix didn't want to be harsh. "Do you think you're ready?"

Jordan jabbed the skinning knife into Gus's eye, deeply enough, and returned the knife to the backpack. "As I'll ever be," he said.

"You sure?" Felix asked, scanning Jordan's appearance.

Jordan became aware of the blood that covered his clothes and skin. "I'd better see if Mr. Merriweather has anything that fits me."

"After..."

"After I check out his shower."

The pants in which Jordan exited the apartment didn't fall down only because he thought to use a necktie like a belt. The shirt overwhelmed his upper body, but the rifle bag kept it from looking too much like a tent. In the lobby, Felix saw that the attendant's blood had indeed pooled in front of the desk, but no one was around. Luck? People might say Father was watching over them.

4. BACCHANAL

Amphitheaters of antiquity were round, but modern ones, like the one in the Settlement of Passing, were more often semicircular. Curved, stepped rows of seats hewn from the earth and covered in slate tile descended to the broad, deep stage area, usually backed by an acoustic shell but sometimes hosting a mountainous movie screen. Behind the stage—today, kept from sight by the acoustic shell—what people had built as a temporary shelter decades ago was now fortified, permanent, the preparation and waiting area, "the sit shack" for the suspenseful hour before what newcomers understood best as "the Bacchanal." Kids who grew up anticipating it called it their "tasting."

The Settlement held the ritual twice per year, on the equinoxes. Felix had waited for his contest, which delayed his tasting. Typically, every new adult, whether new from age or new from joining, participated in the first tasting held during their residency. Being named had forced Felix to wait, but being a True Son wouldn't get Felix out of it this time, not that he wanted out. In fact, when he considered that True Sons were the only ones who could participate more than once, he felt more confident about this time because he'd have a chance, if he needed it, to do better next time. Most True Sons never chose to participate again. Most sat on the dais raised in the amphitheater's center, from which Father watched, and they watched, too.

Most of the Settlement's adult population came to watch from the amphitheater's stony seats. Tonight, the True Son called "Herc" would participate along with the newbies. Excitement levels ran high.

The participation of the newly joined kept Felix among the

youngest of the participants. Lotte, the woman next to him on the bench in the sit shack, was probably ten years older. She'd come from the outside in early summer, recruited from a hospital and fully vetted. Her blonde hair and limbs were long, and most of her was too narrow. Her fake-looking, pink-painted fingernails tapped on her knees. "Do people always die in the Bacchanal?"

"Usually, but not always, I think," Felix said. "Kids aren't allowed. You're not allowed to go *to* one until you've been *through* one, is what people say. They don't talk about it in school. All we hear are rumors."

"I'm in the best shape of my life, but I'm still not used to the exhibitionism," Lotte said.

Exhibitionism. He knew the word and found the concept applied to the Lands' relative lack of attachment to clothing amusing. Everyone in the sit shack was naked, and everyone in the audience, including Father, would be naked. It simply wasn't a clothes-wearing sort of event. Barrels of fire bordered the stage, adding warmth to the area, but it wasn't a cold evening. Who the hell cared about clothes?

Lotte, apparently.

"Do you feel... strange?"

Felix took a gulp from his paper cup full of wine. Eighteen was the drinking age in the Lands, but he hadn't yet taken much advantage of it. Wine was *good.* "Yeah, starting to," he said.

They should have all been feeling strange by now, three other young men close to his age, two young women, all locals. The joiners included five men and eight women, including Lotte. When Herc joined them, they'd be twenty people on stage, a good number for a tasting.

Father had given out the tea, also in paper cups, himself. Salvador walked beside him, carrying the tray as Father handed cups to the evening's participants waiting in the sit shack. "Understand," Father said, "that though you will create a spectacle worth watching, that is only the external manifestation of your experience, which will occupy only a small fraction of your expanded consciousness. Much of your experience will be internal. This ritual is a phenomenon of the mind."

An orgy of the mind.

"Remember that I'm giving each of you your own personal cup of tea. See?" Father held up a cup and pointed to the writing on its side. "Your cup has your name on it. Each cup has the right drug in the right dose for you. Your weight and body chemistry have been considered. Mainly, you're all drinking something chemically almost identical to mescaline, the active component in peyote that makes it a 'vision quest' drug. Those with male libidos get a drug like sildenafil, or Viagra, and those with female libidos get a drug like bremelanotide, or Vyleesi. I've compensated for any nauseating side-effects, and everything should take effect in about an hour, when the ceremony begins. Until then, we have no shortage of wine for you to enjoy. Don't worry—it won't cause complications."

Father was so jovial. Friendly. Real. Felix didn't imagine the Father that was giving out paper cups in the sit shack. The Father that was liked to stay on high. The truly charismatic leader knew how to relate to people.

"Don't worry, Lotte," Felix said. "You'll have a good time."

Even if you die, you'll have a good time.

After Father handed out the tea, Salvador gave participants the only items they would bring on stage. Their bases looked like thimbles, sized for the pinky finger, and they ended with sharp-pointed hooks, arced little claws. They were traditional, people said, meant for pricks of pain and show-damage, but combined with fervor, they could do more. Pluck out an eye. Rip open a throat. Tear scrotum skin or other places where resistance thinned.

Felix smelled the other participants' anxiousness, a blend of sour fear and sweetening appetite. He smelled fire in the darkening air and felt the evening's comfortable crispness on his skin. His mouth tasted hot. Heat trailed down his esophagus to his stomach, joined with his groin. Lotte's pink fingernails tapped on her knees like horses' hooves.

isssssssssssssss tiiiiiiiiiiiiiiiiiiiime

A young woman around his age was staring at him from across the shack. Her eyes, diamond-specked brown, reached from her head and searched him. Her name was Mandy. He'd seen her at night. He'd touched her, and she'd touched him. He licked his teeth.

It'sssssssssss

Commotion! Rising bodies! Skin surrounded him! A man stood, was three separate figures, one on the bench, one getting up, and one standing, all at once, but the sitting one caught up with the rising one, and three became one as he joined the others shambling through wonder toward the shack's front door.

tiiiiiiiiiiiiiiiiime

Brushing her leg against his, a shiver from thigh to heart, Lotte, one, three, six of her, stood, disarrayed, reached for him with several hands, but Felix was smart enough to know the *real* one. "Help help help up up up?" she asked. Her mouth didn't stay still on her face. It traveled. Everything traveled.

Felix took her hand and rose from the bench and found himself in a flesh river, the nineteen bodies from the sit shack pressed together as they shuffled through the door toward the temporary opening in the acoustic shell through which they would pour onstage. The sour smell had given way almost entirely to sweetness, sweetness of skin, sweetness of *want*, rich, musky, intoxicating. His head was light, and the shack was getting brighter, and he couldn't get enough air into his lungs. He reached out and touched the nearest skin, female, male, or otherwise, he didn't care. He touched and touched and realized he was being touched. The mass of people moving to the stage explored each other as they migrated.

BONG! BONG!

The drums began. Big kettle drums on either side of the stage banged in unison.

BONG! BONG! BONG! BONG!

The beginning of the mass must have reached the stage because the audience cheered. The sound wavered, washing around pitches and volumes like they were in a slow blender.

Felix's part of the river—

BONG! BONG!

spilled on stage.

The lights, a semicircle of spotlights around the edge of the stage front, made his hands retreat from the skin surrounding him and grab the sides of his head. At first, he saw the lights themselves, red, blue, and yellow, red, blue, and yellow, red, blue, and yellow, but they beamed in different directions across the stage, intersecting, becoming orange, green, purple, and every combination, color wheels spinning, rolling around the stage, rainbows in his eyes, in his head

he crossed a rainbow bridge, through a rainbow nexus

and the amphitheater was gone

except he still saw it, a man on his knees in front of him, a woman turning his head to one side, pushing her tongue between his lips, a feeling on his back, a scratch sliding down his spine, warm wetness dripped, warm wetness probed between his buttocks

but they were nowhere, and above the stars sat on fading light from the absent sun and grew into manic pinwheels with messages, too many messages at once

death combines all colors

His erection roared.

devoutly to be wished

A man's mouth bobbed on his cock. A woman's lips enveloped his; their tongues rubbed one another. His hands massaged her tits with the rhythm of his own throbbing pulse. Behind him, someone licked his asshole and lapped at the blood dripping from the scratch along his spine. Heaven—

consolation for those too fragile for death's incomprehensible magnitude

Pleasure, ecstasy.

the explosion of comprehension was ecstasy

A million stars overhead exploded in incomprehensible spectrums.

Hands, pinky hooks visible but not digging in, grabbed the

shoulders of the man on Felix's cock, pulled the man back, and shoved him to the stage floor. A woman had him. She straddled him. She rode his cock, and Felix couldn't tell whether the man was moaning or screaming.

Not far from where the woman rode the blowjob man, a small table with a bowl on top was flanked by paper cups. Similar bowls were scattered around the stage. More wine. Leaving sensations and the woman he was kissing behind, Felix lurched for more wine, splashed some into his mouth and some on his bare chest. In the evening light, red wine looked more like blood than usual. Already, the tasting participants looked covered in blood.

Scratch. Scratch.

He almost couldn't feel someone's pinky hook slashing his forearm, but he dropped his paper cup and looked around. Mandy, with the brown eyes specked with diamonds like the spinning stars, loomed near with a giggle the noise of which got eaten by

BONG! BONG! BONG! BONG!

Always drumming, syncing heartbeats, throbbing, marching, driving them on. Felix stepped toward her.

A man, one of the older ones, grabbed the back of her long black hair and pulled her to him. He jammed fingers between her legs and looked like he stuck her entire chin in his mouth. His pinky hook scratched at her ass while his other hand stabbed into her vagina.

Felix felt a splash from behind. One of the young men, Ryan, who'd had a birthday after Felix but not been named, had tossed a cupful of wine on Felix's already dripping back. His round face opened in a gleeful laugh and got wider, wider, and wider, a bright moon guffawing. A surge of affection for Ryan and everyone made Felix go to the next nearest wine bowl, dip in a cup, and splash the young man, then splash the woman standing near him, then drop the cup and put both hands in the bowl to splash, splash, splash anyone he could reach.

Laughter echoed, echoed, and bare flesh bent, warped with the flowing wine and blood, people embracing, scratching, laughing, biting, and finally licking. They licked the wine from each other's skin. Before Felix understood, he licked, too, and he tasted plums and cherries and grapes and pepper and chocolate and earth and the copper of blood that blended it all. Licking turned into biting, which broke skin like the pinky hooks, front teeth, incisors, gasps, gushes. A man yelped when a woman bit down on his penis, but his face showed ecstasy.

BONG! BONG!

Firelight orange and all the crazy primaries dancing and having spectrums of light children that flickered and swarmed around the stage with people coupling and decoupling and forming threesomes and foursomes and piles that congealed and dispersed, congealed and dispersed. Felix felt heat pump from all the bodies around him, sweat, sweet but grungy, the stink of secretions of bodies grinding, cocks entering pussies and assholes and any place they could find, the stars spitting down on them, the world a rain of fluids.

The audience cheered. Felix thought they reflected the enthusiasm he felt for the rain of color, the rain of wine and blood and sweat and come, didn't know if he'd come but knew he was hard and felt like he would always be hard because he channeled the stuff of the universe, a conduit of sex
bodies

BONG! BONG!

But he saw, at first like a pack of nude, thick-muscled men, then like an individual, Herc, one of the youngest True Sons, descend the dais, march down through the cheering rows, and strut into the stage's swirling throng to a wine bowl, where he dipped in a paper cup, the contents of which he guzzled before he dipped it in again and dumped the red liquid on his face, bringing the applause to a peak.

A woman Felix recognized, Belinda, with curly brown hair and pillowy breasts, threw herself at Herc. He caught her, kissed her, and pushed her away. She charged him again, and he caught her again, pushed her head back, and drew a line with his pinky hook from her forehead down her cheek to her chin. Faint red blossomed in the line, and Belinda screamed, "YES!"

Treatments would follow the tasting, but many people had scars from their tasting that lasted for the rest of their lives, markers on their

bodies

In the dance of colors, all the frantic bodies, licking, sucking, kneading, fucking—they looked colorless. Drained. Herc knocked the wine bowl he had used from its tabletop. The bowl hit the back of a man on top of a woman whose legs wrapped around his waist. Red drenched them, but the impact didn't slow his thrusts. Herc lifted Belinda so she sat on the edge of the cleared table. He leaned her back, supporting her weight by holding her hands, and slipped his cock inside her. She yelled when he thrust.

Flesh moved around Felix in flashes. Lips closed on erect nipples. Each time a nearby woman's head moved down the shaft of a man's penis, her pinky hook cut another tally mark into the man's flat chest. The drums banged the same persistent beat, but participants' movements became more and more hyperkinetic, reaching for one person, then another, this cock, that pussy, any part, every part, flesh, flesh, flesh.

Nothing but bodies. Drained of color, drained of significance. Pleasure was a sickness.

An orgy of the mind.

Because the scratches on his back and arm and the tingling rushes from between his legs were all the same. The body was a prison, but the mind was, too.

Sex was death because death required living and living required death.

He felt cool fingers wrap around his penis. They guided him into a warmer place.

His mind stayed with the stars, spinning stars, exploding and exploded into color that made the bodies as gray as corpses. Because they *were* corpses. The stars that shined brightest were already dead. In glory on the stage, they all waited for their deaths to be realized.

Father's wisdom.

Blood and wine covered the stage. Felix realized that he stood pressed against Mandy, fucking her. He licked his teeth. He'd never been inside a woman this way before. It felt good. It felt like death, the inside of the womb.

His mind discorporated again, and he saw the dais, Father at center, naked, holding binoculars, as erect as he'd been when his cock had been in Felix's mouth. He stroked himself. Father stroked himself, watching the stage, and Salvador watched him. Salvador's eyes followed Father's hand as it stroked Father's cock, and his eyes followed Father's eyes, the direction of his gaze toward the stage. His gaze toward Felix.

"PLEASE STOP! I CAN'T DO THIS! I NEED TO GO HOME! LET ME OUT! PLEASE, LET ME OUT!"

BONG! BONG! BONG! BONG!

The woman's voice screaming to be let out snapped Felix's attention back to his body, the stage, and what was happening within all the colors of death. Mandy was gone. Lotte, narrow chest, narrow waist, narrow hips Lotte, blonde hair spread in a fan over her head, lay on the stage in front of him. She twisted and thrashed. She extended and flailed her arms as a defense against anyone who might come near.

"STOP!" she wailed. Her arms, legs, tits, and face had gashes, as if more than one person had dug into her skin with pinky hooks, gashes that bled like pouring wine. "I WANT TO GO HOME!"

Lotte would never go to a home that wasn't the Settlement of Passing. Adults could come and go, but joiners could never return to their old lives, especially if they were frightened by a ritual. The people of the Nothing Lands kept their secrets. The last time someone had gone to the media about a "death cult," the Settlement had gone into lockdown for months. Thoughts of imprisonment made Felix feel cold.

Death cult.

Death *culture.*

Death *cultivation.*

Felix found himself on top of Lotte, slamming his cock into

her vaginal opening, smashing his pelvis against hers, wanting their bones to break. His cock slipped out, covered in blood, and he slid back in, thrusting harder than before.

BONG! BONG! BONG!

Lotte screamed, but the stage was a chorus of screams. A chorus of colorless corpses painted in blood and wine. Lotte slapped at him with her flailing arms, and he pierced her with greater fury. Bodies, meaningless, absurd bodies. He could tear off Lotte's arms like Marianne tore off Darlene's. Herc could knock off Belinda's head like a blood-filled doll's.

A weight pressed down from behind him, followed by a pain that rolled from his backside through his guts and up to his mouth. The sensation resolved, and he thought he knew what was happening before he craned his neck around to look.

Herc wasn't with Belinda anymore. On his knees, Herc was behind him, leaning forward so his dick stayed in Felix's ass. Felix's vision, already confused by the parts of Lotte that multiplied and refused to stay still, blurred with the pain of the intrusion where he'd never allowed or intended to allow anyone. He felt like he could turn inside out. No, he didn't want this feeling, didn't want Herc to fuck him any more than Lotte wanted to be here or have Felix on top of her, but desire was not the universe's operational principle.

Herc rammed his cock into Felix, and Felix rammed his cock into Lotte. Felix moved back and forth, his parts enveloping and enveloped by theirs. The sensation wasn't unpleasant.

Riding it, Felix looked at Father, who stroked himself at double the pace of the drums. Salvador looked morose as he monitored the spectacle on the dais and the spectacle on the stage.

The sensation ended abruptly when Herc pulled out of Felix's ass and pushed him off Lotte. Felix rolled onto his back, dizzy, legs quivering, stars above spinning with all the colors the bodies lacked. He tried to sit up and got far enough to see Herc straddle Lotte's face and fuck her mouth with his dirty dick. Vomit leaked from the corners of her lips, but not much escaped. Her eyes rolled up into her head.

Two of the older men, the joiner men, lifted Herc by the armpits, or so Felix concluded. One of them looked ten feet tall, the other much smaller, and between them, Herc looked like stretched taffy. Felix thought he heard words beneath the *BONG! BONG! BONG! BONG!*, but he couldn't make out the argument. He did see one of the joiner men point downstage, and there, disarranged, was Belinda, slashed this way and that, twirling in eddies but devoid of her own movement. Felix understood. Herc had killed her, and Lotte was dead as well.

bodies

Participants seemed to care. As far as Felix knew, the rules weren't against it—weren't against caring—even if the cold stars were.

Those on their feet, eight or ten maybe, women and men, gathered around the two men who held up the struggling Herc. They all had bleeding scratches—Felix hadn't expected the hooks to leave so many marks—and some had major wounds. Blood and wine, wine and blood. The spotlights beamed spectrums but seemed irrelevant. All that mattered was red and the pallor of absence.

An unexpected death seemed soon to be realized, and the audience was silent.

On the dais, a flurry of activity divided the audience's attention from the figures closing in on Herc. Most of the True Sons rose from their seats, and given their inability to hold a consistent size or shape, Felix doubted what he saw, but they seemed to produce swords from nowhere and shout about what their distorted body language suggested might be rushing the stage to come to Herc's rescue.

This tasting, this Bacchanal, this ritual of sex and death, would become pure slaughter, participants falling in pieces at the True Sons' feet. The True Sons held back while they looked where Felix looked, to Father. Father's face remained expressionless as the audience's silence united with its attention, both absolute in deference to the man who remained seated, calm, and unarmed while those around him appeared agitated enough for war. Father looked to his True Sons on one side and then on the other. He raised his hands, palms flat, parallel to the dais. He pressed downward through empty air. The True Sons understood. They retook their seats.

Charismatic.

The two men on stage still held Herc by his underarms, and everyone knew now that no one was going to intervene on Herc's behalf.

Another one of the men, Nestor, who had become an adult in the Settlement without being named, walked on shaky, bleeding feet—he might have been missing toes—to stand between Herc and the audience, to face Herc directly. Overcoming the resistant jerks of Herc's neck, he used both hands to pry open Herc's jaw.

Mandy took a place beside him and stuck her right hand, pinky hook first, into Herc's mouth. Felix couldn't see what happened inside, but he heard Herc's open-mouthed squeal as his tongue extended beyond his teeth and lips. Mandy had the back of the tongue on her hook, and she worked the hook through its thickness. The men at Herc's armpits tightened their grip as Mandy pulled the tongue out and forward, blood on Herc's chin, blood on his chest and stomach, blood on the stage in front of him. The squealing got louder, but Mandy kept his tongue from assisting. On her hook, it only extended, and it tore in the middle as she pulled. It split. She pulled until the hook broke free through the tongue's tip. Herc's tongue lolled outside his mouth, forked and spilling red.

Nestor backed off, and other men and women closed in on Herc, taking their pinky hooks to other parts of his face. A hook went into the soft skin beneath the left eye and tore it open, pulling through the lump of cheek below. Someone clawed at the nose, tearing apart both nostrils, ripping skin until cartilage showed. A hook caught the right eye near the pupil—pluck!—but the sound Felix imagined he heard was more of a squelch than a pop. He wondered how he saw so much and realized he was on his feet, or he floated, either way no longer lying on the ground, risen with others who watched the main group clawing at Herc. At some point, enough scratches had made Herc cross a line into not having a face, only ribbons.

The group of participants that surrounded Herc was no longer composed of individuals, only a mass, and flesh-wearing amoeba absorbing its prey. Felix floated, and the mass, bulging and withdrawing in shifting places along its curved edges, brought Herc to the stage floor, on his back.

BONG! BONG!

Felix floated and watched the body. Father watched. The other True Sons watched their brother absorbed by death, the equality of all flesh. *Within* that equality, the blur of skin tones into one, Felix saw what wasn't there. The woman sitting on the tatters of Herc's face held his forked tongue, three times as long as it should have been, cut from its root in the bottom of his mouth, incapable of retraction, and rubbed it up and down between her labia, occasionally teasing her clit. She faced another woman who straddled Herc's hips, impaled on his cock, hard enough to ride even though the amoeba body was devouring him, incorporating him.

Many arms with hands with pinky hooks came out of the body and scratch-scratch-scratched like trapped rats' feet, burrowing. In a flash Felix thought he saw a man shove his cock into Herc's chest and thought *lungfucker* and chuckled, but that couldn't be, yet extraordinary empathy enveloped his own aching erection in quivering silky softness, either extraordinary empathy or maybe he *was* the lungfucker. He chuckled. Was he part of the bigger body? He didn't know anymore. Burrowers breached Herc's well-toned abs and broke into his stomach, but they didn't pull the insides out. They tunneled.

One or two people tunneled into Herc's legs, too. A woman who had figured out how to use her pinky hook like a drill, careful not to scrape the ass of the woman sitting on Herc's ex-face, tunneled into Herc's skull.

An urge to drink Herc's blood made Felix uncomfortable.

The body permeated Herc, penises and fingers and tongues

exploring holes that had been and holes that were made, and Herc seemed to realize death didn't stop the crowded fucking because death and the body were indistinct. Felix understood that he was part of the body and always had been, always indistinct, always insignificant. Only Father reached farther.

The body focused on its living parts, writhing, stroking, filling the readymade holes, finding pleasure. No other death was realized during the tasting. Orgiastic minds drifted into unconsciousness.

Father watched from his position on the dais, from his position between the body and the stars.

5. THE PURITY OF TRANSGRESSION

First House didn't aspire to ostentation but was big and impressive enough to be called a palace, with the high ceilings in the public dining and meeting rooms and the black carpet and fragmented sculptures in the grand receiving hall where the dais spent most of its time. In the back of the building, the wing adjacent to the grow house was devoted entirely to laboratories and examination rooms, and across the building's divided central corridor, the front of which was the receiving hall, the back of which was for private meetings of Father and Sons, the opposite wing hosted a menagerie, a place for animals to live when they didn't have roles in the labs.

Midway between the public front and very private, very *secret* back were the wings for living quarters. One wing hosted the True Sons with lavish accommodations, which Felix appreciated even more after seeing Gus Merriweather's "studio." He supposed his quarters were a studio as well, but he had twice the space, a full living room set facing one TV while his king-sized bed faced another, and an actual kitchen with a dishwasher and a refrigerator as tall as he was. Yes, until this point in life he had always lived in dormitories with roommates... and not every adult got the benefits of being a True Son... but outside never won by any measure. Outside would never escape the quagmire of its confusion. Too many people called themselves believers without knowing what they believed.

The wing opposite the True Sons' quarters belonged to

Father. It included a room for sacrifices. It included rooms for other activities Father found pleasing. No one entered without Father's direct invitation.

When Father appeared in his doorway a few hours before dawn a week after Felix's tasting, Felix expected he would deliver an invitation to a sacrifice, perhaps even a charge to be executioner. "Good, um, morning, Father." They didn't emphasize protocol in First House, but it did exist, and Felix didn't know whether he should somehow acknowledge the honor of being singled out for a visit.

Father was as casual as his loose white pants cinched at the waist and his bare upper body. "Sorry to get you out of bed."

"You—sorry... no. I...."

"Would you come for a walk with me?" Father asked as if Felix might say no.

"Of course! Give me a...." Felix left Father in the doorway and ran to collect a pair of white pants in the same style as Father's, pants he almost ripped apart as he teetered stepping into them. He slipped into sandals and ran back to the doorway. "Anywhere you want to go!"

Father smiled in an indulgent way that made Felix feel like he was back in the nursery. He didn't care, though. Father had asked him to go for a walk.

Again, he failed to anticipate what Father had in mind. Felix imagined staying in the palatial house, maybe taking a tour of the menagerie or labs. He dared to hope he might see the grow house, but his mind went no farther out. The short walk to the exit at the end of the True Sons' wing disappointed him at first, then swept him into new speculation about where they could be going and why.

The night remained dark. Not much of a moon, and the sun was hours off.

At a deliberate pace, Father led Felix to the edge of the woods, not the thicket of trees you passed through to get to the dirt circle, but the actual woods. The Nothing Lands included the Settlement of Passing, hundreds of acres of farmland, and hundreds of acres of woodland—Felix didn't know how big it all was; he only knew that fences, with defenses, surrounded the whole area. Within, the woods could seem to go on forever, and the trails within them, squiggled and layered like spaghetti, reinforced the effect. At the edge where trees began, Father finally spoke: "You know the woods?"

"I used to be play in them," Felix said. "Everybody does, but… not at night."

"The woods are scary at night, aren't they?"

He didn't need to lie to Father. "Yes."

"Good! Let's go."

Father led into the woods. Felix looked at his broad shoulders, gray in the dim night. Inside the trees, even the white of his pants would be hard to see. Felix followed. Father wasn't divine or invincible. He often reminded people of his mortality, discouraging worship. But being by Father's side, Felix felt safe. Protected. Father was stronger than the dark.

"Fear is purifying," Father said. Felix could barely see Father or the path in front of them. Trees around them were shapeshifting, shadowy walls. Leaves and nettles susurrated in the breeze. Father's steps had the same deliberation as they had on the way over, where treetops hadn't colluded to hide the sky's small light. Maybe he didn't need to see where they were going. Felix stayed close to Father's side. "Every fear is a sample of the greatest fear."

"What's that?" Felix felt stupid. "Death, I suppose."

"Not exactly," Father said. "It's what you feel in confrontation with the void. Death people have spent millennia storying away, staving it off with fictions of afterlives and resurrections. Total absence, though… total negation… that's the rush. If fear is a high, that's the greatest peak. Try as you might, you can't imagine your own nullity. You're always there to perceive that you're not there. The priests used to claim that God is the infinite the human mind cannot fathom. I'll show you centuries upon centuries of art and literature fathoming until you puke! But I can't show you one picture of the void. The closest attempts would be solid black or solid white, but neither would come close to it. It evades representation because it explodes comprehension."

The explosion of comprehension was ecstasy.

Felix tripped on a root he couldn't have seen in the obscure path, fell forward, and sensed the ground coming to splat against his face. Father caught him, set him upright. "Here," he said with an offer of his elbow's crook, "take my arm."

Felix did.

"Fear purifies because it offers a taste of self-annihilation. Pain and sex purify for the same reason, in varying degrees. At a certain point of suffering, or a certain peak of pleasure, consciousness ceases, and the self nearly evaporates. The void was very present during your time on stage at the amphitheater."

"I felt everything but was surrounded by nothing," Felix said.

"Yes. Tell me, Felix. Do you like pain?"

Felix thought of the scratch on his back, not fully healed. It still irritated him when he bent or twisted. That wasn't real pain, though. Hugo, on the other hand, had hurt him. He'd needed time to recover. During the fight, pain had kept him alert, pushed him forward. He hadn't thought about liking it.
During private times at school, he'd cut himself to feel the hurt. A lot of kids did. Teachers approved. "Sometimes," Felix answered.

Father laughed. "At least you're honest, and you're more receptive than most. When more than half the residents reach the end of their journeys, they ask me to let them go in their sleep, as if sleep were already a step in the direction of abnegation. I let them go. We are compassionate here. Individuals don't have family or careers or the usual stresses that create false longings for death. We exist in constant, personal negotiation with our endings, in preparation for the confrontation with the void, and if the outcome of someone's negotiation is death in sleep, I will facilitate, even though I admire those who seize the confrontation as the apex of experience, the cathartic climax of emotion. Don't you?"

Had Herc come to the stage planning to end his journey? "I do," Felix said. He didn't want to die in his sleep.

"After I became a True Son, I went to the outside a lot," Father said. Father never spoke of the time before he was realized as Father. "I wore clothes I shouldn't have worn in places I shouldn't have visited. I said things to men I shouldn't have spoken to until I finally provoked them. They used billy clubs and baseball bats and tire irons while shouting 'faggot' and other words we don't have much use for here. Typically, I scared them off with my laughter. They got scared when they couldn't beat the smile off my face."

Felix could imagine a younger Father, beaten but still powerful, and he nodded even though he didn't think Father could see him nod. "Outside is hateful," Felix said.

"Their hate makes them easy to manipulate. But that's neither here nor there. I enjoyed hobbling back to the Settlement, bashed, bruised, bloody, broken-boned. The brothers and sisters took care of me. They said I came close to dying more than once. I reveled in it. I felt more connected to everyone. I knew pain better, so I knew *their* pain better."

They moved together, but Felix had no awareness of walking. He heard.

"I have a memory I want to share with you. A girl, fourteen, decided she'd reached the end. As I'm sure you know, children who believe they're at the time for death will receive support if they pass an interview, which this girl did. She made a special request, though, not unprecedented in adults but a first from a child, and it caused a stir.

"*End assist.* An end assist could be someone sticking a needle in your vein for you, or it could be someone pulling a trigger, or it could be someone chopping you into itty bitty bits. This girl wasn't merely problematic because she was a child but because she was a *creative* child. She wanted multiple people to assist, quite rare. Four people. Each one had to find a hefty branch in these woods. The branches didn't have to be smooth, but they had to be of a size and weight for swinging.

"Residents didn't jump at the opportunity to assist. True Sons had to step in, which thrilled the girl, who had also requested that the event occur in the dirt circle, where women never knew pain or death. Was she making a statement? Rebelling? I don't know. I do know she wanted four people to beat her to death with tree branches. I knew what ecstasy in battery felt like, and I wanted to see her feel it. I didn't care where it happened.

"The same masses too squeamish to volunteer assistance showed up in droves to watch. The naked girl stood in the dirt circle's center, and the four Sons made a square around her, heavy branches resting on their bare shoulders. What do you know about sadism?"

Felix reflected. "Fucking Lotte on stage, I wanted to break her." He'd wanted them both to break.

"The desire to inflict pain is altruistic, and all True Sons must cultivate it."

Death cultivation.

"My Sons knew not to make the process quick, and I think the girl expected them to take their time. On the dais, through my binoculars, I studied her face. Not a smile, but pleasing serenity. She didn't seem to sense the crowd around her. She faced the void and looked serene.

"Of course, when the first man stepped forward and swung at her, her face swirled from serenity to panic, and she jumped sideways, toward a different man, to dodge. The man now closest to her swept her lower legs from beneath her, and she hit the dirt. The man who had swung and missed grabbed one of her feet and dragged her back to the center of the circle, where another man kept her from sitting up by stomping on her shoulder. The True Sons surrounded her, and the only man who hadn't touched her got them started with a whack of his branch against her feet. I heard the crack and saw one foot twist in a way it wasn't supposed to. The girl shouted, 'Oh!'

"The men took their time, almost an hour. Each struck her feet until bones poked through skin in all directions. They pulverized her calves, her thighs. She looked like polychromatic blue puzzle pieces that didn't fit together. By the time they broke apart her head she probably felt nothing. I mostly watched her face, though. It showed the pain when she cried out, 'Oh!,' but in the lulls between strikes, it struggled to reform the image of serenity. Somewhere she confronted the void, edged toward it, and she had power. She didn't rage. She didn't retreat. With her body shattered by her own will, she walked into the void."

"Sounds like a saint," Felix said. He didn't know what to think.

Father laughed, pulled Felix closer, and tousled his hair with a hand Felix couldn't see. "There are no saints and martyrs, but if there were saints and martyrs, she'd be one or the other or both. You're smart, you know?"

"Thank you." Felix's heart beat faster.

"You and I could work together," Father said.

Felix, stunned, stopped walking, but Father didn't, so Felix felt his pull and moved on, saying, "What?"

"We could be a team."

"I'm already yours, I—"

"A Father with many Sons chooses favorites."

They walked in pitch black silence.

Charismatic. What if every True Son shared a secret with Father? What if every True Son thought he was a, or even the, "favorite?" Father needed to be father of all.

"I don't know why I'd deserve that honor," Felix said.

Father hmphed, jovially. "Because all my other True Sons assume they deserve it without questioning why? That's part of the reason, anyway. Because I see a lot of me in you. Because you're smart. Because a Father needs an heir."

Felix reflected. He needed to be careful. From books he knew that palaces bred palace intrigue. "What about Salvador?"

"Salvador is something else to me. He is fit for devotion. You have different aptitudes."

"I am devoted—"

"Of course you are."

Did Father think he wasn't devoted to him? To the Settlement of Passing? To the Nothing Lands?

"You never asked me why the True Sons must cultivate sadism," Father said.

Fighting back the paranoia, Felix focused on sadism. "I assumed you meant that sharing pain is a virtue because pain is a means of self-abnegation."

Father's reaction was invisible. They were two invisible men, floating voices prickled by the occasional breezy gust and tickled by the sounds of movement in the trees. "Okay, what you said, and hurting someone is a transgression. Hurting yourself is a transgression. Especially for those of us raised here in the Lands, the transgressiveness of our primary principles, of our reason for being, can be easy to forget because we think so differently from outsiders."

When Felix had drilled Jordan with rote Q&A to keep him calm and settled for his practice sacrifice, Jordan had been able to deliver mechanistic answers because he was prepared. Felix ought to have been prepared for this question of transgression, but he didn't have an answer for it, didn't have the key to unlock what Father was telling him, and he felt so much lesser.

"What brings us together is that everyone here rejects what the scientific regime of the outside regards as the most fundamental, defining motivator of the human species: survival. We transgress their basic values because while they base their society on their desire to survive, we base ours on our desire *not* to."

Felix understood.

"Outside, deliberately denying children experience of family would be transgressive, and that's one reason we do it. Outside, spectacles of carnage, at least those that go as far as human death, would be transgressive, and that's one reason why we have them. Outside," Father laughed, "healthcare and equal opportunities for all would be transgressive, but that's just a bonus, because we have them so people don't get distracted by unnecessary inequalities on their journeys toward death."

Felix reflected. "Outsiders are kind of backward, aren't

they?"

"Most people aren't stupid. They're misled. But we purify ourselves by transgressing the values—not only the values, the *perceptions*—of the world that surrounds our Lands. We embrace the beauty of ugliness. We embrace the life of death."

Felix reflected, the only awareness of his body the giddiness he felt in his stomach. "Tell me, Father. What's the team of you and me going to do first?"

6. UNTRUE

Every guy wanted to fuck a pregnant girl. Outside the schools, vaginal sex wasn't forbidden, but it was stigmatized, especially if it led to pregnancy and thus abortion. Unscheduled conceptions disrupted the order of living and dying, everyone knew. Women who were out of service and had abortions were trash. Everyone knew. Pregnancy meant no risk of conception, no risk of condemnation. Pregnant women enjoyed recreational selection.

Trotski seemed to be offering him whatever kind of sex he wanted. The offer intrigued him. She had a bubble in the middle, not the huge bulges he'd seen with Darlene and Beth, and the shapes of her breasts would feel good in his hands. Thinking about slipping between her legs made his crotch ache. She was a good ache.

Not a good person. Father had warned him.

"Thank you for meeting me," Trotski said. Her shirt had a plain, simple cut, white fabric draping around her breasts to midriff, and her basic skirt, the match to Felix's basic pants, hung to her knees. The brown skin of her lower legs, arms, and bubble belly had a hazy glow in the firelight, flickering with it. "They tell me you're smart."

"They're very kind," Felix said. The evening was too warm for a campfire, but two people chatting at a campfire a little off the trail in the late evening would attract no attention. The burning logs were ornamental, not practical.

They added mystique.

To be practical, Felix had strapped his folded knife with the three-inch serrated blade over his right ankle, under the bottom rim of his pants leg. He might not need to share this bit of practicality with anyone, but he was prepared.

"Do you know why I asked you to come here?" Trotski put a finger by the corner of her mouth.

"You're implying it's not my physical attractions." Felix gestured to his shirtless physique.

"How smart are you?"

"I get by."

"Smart enough to think for yourself?"

"Since when is that always smart?"

"Hmm," she said. "Fair point." Shadows made myriad grays on her white clothes and brown skin and dripped from her long, black hair. "Tell me. Do you expect to be at the end of your journey five months from now?"

Felix folded his arms across his chest. "I hadn't given it any thought."

"Do you want to be dead in five months? Yes or no."

"If it would please—"

"YES OR NO!"

"No," Felix said, not sensing a right answer. "I have unfinished business."

"So do I," Trotski said, "but I've got a fifty percent chance of dying in five months when this thing gets pulled out of me, and I don't like those odds. I got lucky once. I don't think I'll be lucky again."

Trotski had grown up in the Settlement, so, being on her second pregnancy, she had to be older—twenty-two? He detected maturity in her manner. They could fuck on the ground beside the fire, and no one would care. Felix needed to remember that he'd agreed to meet her because suspicions needed verification. Her purpose went beyond sex. "What do you want from me?" he asked, not too eager, not too gruff.

"Are you smart enough to think that killing women who give birth to boys is... crazy? Nonsensical? Unnecessary?"

The only rationality in life was death. Ritual was necessary for concentration. Ritual was necessary because it was ritual. Felix said, "Tell me what you're thinking."

Effusing trepidation, she said, "Things... could... change."

"You want me to join you so we can revolutionary agents of change? In a weird way, I'm honored."

"No," she said with continuing care. "Not... just... me. Can I trust you?"

"I'm a pretty trustworthy guy, I think people—"

"YES OR NO! If I share a secret, will you keep it?"

Felix pretended to consider. "Yes," he said. He made a contemplative face. "Things could change."

Trotski led him away from the fire—still burning, so she must have planned on coming back—and before long, her direction revealed their destination: the amphitheater. They entered from the stage side, accessing the stage from between parts of the acoustic shell, as Felix had for his tasting, so the first thing Felix saw, or didn't see, were the rounded steps of the audience. A wall of light hit him hard, halting his entrance. Around the rear of the theater and in places throughout, white spotlights pointed toward the stage, turning the seating area into a blinding mass. In the lowest rows, Felix made out indistinct figures, uncountable because they blurred together, and his vision went splotchy if he looked toward the audience too long. He could tell that the figures didn't have faces, though. Masks, white porcelain tragedy masks to go with the form-concealing white fabric of the ceremonial robes. Unknown people, unknown numbers.

By contrast that Felix presumed was deliberate, the figures on the bright stage were naked and known. Closest to the round metal tub at center stood Salvador, dark curly hair, olive-toned skin, puffy lips, sculpted torso and legs, severed woman's head held up by its long blonde hair in his right hand. The neck, from which vertebrae protruded, dripped red, but not enough to account for the wide streaks on Salvador's skin.

Felix could smell and taste burning. His eyes burned. The air carried a faint waft of rot.

Stage right of Salvador sat three large wooden chests, and

near them stood Gill, Mister, and Eugene, three more of the True Sons, blood-streaked like Salvador. Two more streaked True Sons, Benjy and Orion, stood stage left, perhaps for balance. That made six. Six of the eight other "True" Sons who remained. Puck and Joffy weren't accounted for.

"This isn't about all women, and this isn't about changing our fundamental way of life. We have structures for good reasons. We have rituals. Living requires dying." Salvador dropped the severed head into the metal tub. Felix heard a loud hiss and saw steam or smoke rise from the tub. The smells of burning and rot got stronger as whatever was in the tub sizzled, bubbled.

Consumed.

Father had a formula for a liquid more potent than simple acids, more effective for dissolving what needed to be dissolved. Quicker than cremation and more certain to destroy all identifiable traces.

Mister took a mannish-looking lower leg, foot attached, from his wooden chest and brought it to Salvador. It dripped a trail across the stage. The people in the chests had been hacked into portability not long ago.

"We're talking about balance in our journeys, balance between women and men in the Settlement of Passing. A change, yes, but one more than offset with the outsiders' sacrifices that will accompany the births of sons *and* daughters." PLOP! HISS! The calf-and-foot went into the tub and sizzled.

Balance. Salvador talked about *balance* when six of the nine True Sons fomented rebellion against an order established by vision beyond his ken. Balance? Unbalanced! Father provided balance because Father provided vision, and what Salvador proposed—

"How do we enact the change we need?" Orion asked. "How do we achieve balance?"

Felix looked at Orion, then blinded himself with a glance toward the audience. How many people? How many people were tempted by this treachery?

The look on Salvador's face, during Felix's tasting—

"We must confront Father," Salvador said.

Salvador had Father's ear. He could speak with him about anything. He needed a "we" to "confront" Father because he knew talk wouldn't get him what he wanted.

A Father needs an heir.

Salvador was recruiting an attack force.

Salvador, who was *something else* to Father.

Salvador, who took a handful of droopy viscera from Gill and a hand from Eugene and tossed them into the dissolving liquid, which sloshed over the tub's rim, reddish-green. The air felt toxic. Salvador continued to demonstrate his ritual that would *offset* what had pleased the Father that was and continued to please Father. As if Salvador knew better than Father.

Treason. Blasphemy. Such words made new sense.

Felix nudged Trotski and said, "I think I've seen enough. I think I understand."

"Okay, then."

He and Trotski had stayed by the acoustic shell, on the stage's border, and they slipped away without drawing any apparent notice or disrupting the steady dissolution of disaggregated people, already mixed and mismatched in the wooden chests before they got disintegrated into an inedible broth that could in no way replace a boy's need to eat his mother. Salvador indulged in silliness, not true transgression, with his soup display.

He would pay.

Trotski led Felix back to the fire where they'd started. It had calmed to embers but radiated enough orange to enhance the glow of Trotski's skin. "Are you with us?" she asked.

"Let me kiss you." Felix liked kissing. Girls, boys, didn't matter. Sloppy wet mouths touching instead of talking. Lips, soft flesh like the body's insides peeking outside, pressing against each other. Tongues probing tongues, cheeks, a tickle at the teeth. Lips pressing *hard*. Trotski let him push his face into hers, winding left and right as he lowered her, strong arm supporting her back, to the ground beside the embers. "Salvador seems smart, doesn't he?"

"Yeah," Trotski said.

Felix pushed her shirt up to her neck and took one breast in each hand, squeezing, exploring the curves with his fingertips, squeezing again. She must have been a wet nurse for a year or so after her first pregnancy. There wouldn't be milk now, but to suck on one of those nipples then... he sucked one now, nibbled it, licked around the areola. He repeated with the other nipple to make sure it wouldn't feel left out. The embers were making him sweat. Maybe the waves of heat would have been running over him anyway. The stiffness below his cinched waistband tried to burst through fabric. He kissed between her breasts, down toward the little bubble belly. "I think you're smart, too," he said.

She moaned and said, "Balance. Balance so we can focus on the journey."

He wanted to scream at the whore, SELF-ABNEGATION ISN'T SELFISH! Instead, he raised her arms and lifted her shirt the rest of the way off. He balled the fabric and set it near her head before rubbing her arms and the sides of her breasts, before resuming his path of kisses along her belly.

As he pulled her skirt all the way down, off over her feet, he said, "Salvador is smart, you're smart, and I'm smart." After lowering his own pants, freeing his erection, he launched up over Trotski so his eyes hovered over hers, and he caged her upper body with his arms. Drained of affect, he said, "We're all so fucking smart."

Her body tensed beneath him. Keeping distance with arms mostly straight, he crawled downward, but before he seemed about to bury his face between her legs, he pulled back on his knees. The repositioning was awkward, and several times Trotski looked like she might say something. When Felix moved her legs so that she bent them at the knees and spread, she resisted at first, then relaxed. On his knees, he sat as close to her as he could. He lifted her ass with his left hand until her pelvis was at the right height to meet his. He slid his cock inside her, willing himself not to come right away. She was tight. Not as tight as an asshole, but tighter than he'd expected, maybe because of the fear. The tense muscles and trembling gave her away. She didn't trust him.

He slid in and out, savoring distrust, keeping his right hand free.

"You being with us means everything." Her voice had pleasure in it.

"Everything," Felix repeated. He'd hammered into Lotte, trying to break her. But Herc had killed her, right? He hadn't killed her. Had he? Did it matter? He wanted to kill Trotski.

"You mean everything," the pregnant woman said.

With his free right hand, Felix grabbed the folded knife strapped to his leg. He unfolded the blade with his thumb. He smiled at Trotski. "Nothing means anything," he said.

"What?" she said. Stupid bitch!

Felix didn't need any more motivation. He brought his blade down in an arc from above his shoulder and rammed it into the woman's waistline, above the main triangle of pubic hair but below the navel. Blood spurted. She started to scream, but Felix was quick. He left the knife sticking out of the wound, grabbed the shirt by her head, and shoved it into her mouth, blocking sound. Some of her shock-terror-desperation noise made its way into the night air, but not enough of it got out to attract anyone's attention.

The woman's fight distracted him from the mounting need to let his cock explode inside her. One of her hands reached for the improvised gag, but Felix ignored it to grab the knife from her midsection, which her other hand was trying to retrieve. He slashed the forearm of the hand on the gag and stabbed the hand that had been close to the knife. The stabbed hand retreated immediately, but the other kept going for the gag, so Felix slashed it twice more, and one of the slashes cut deeply. Trotski's arms collapsed, defeated, and Felix kept fucking her.

He didn't waste time, though, before reinserting his blade in the gushing wound he'd made in her waistline. As if he'd pressed a button, both of her hands clapped toward his knife hand. Responding by reflex, his left arm abandoned its position holding up her ass, so he dropped her the short distance so that she was flat on the ground again, and his dick slipped out. His right hand jerked the knife upward from the waistline wound, splitting skin and layers underneath up to the bellybutton, before he pulled out the blade and lashed at her hands, scoring knuckles and slicing off skin. She tried to wriggle away, but since they weren't fucking anymore, he could pin her more easily with his legs and left arm.

His right hand went back to cutting a vertical line into her belly bubble. It was the opposite of what he'd seen Marianne do in the clinic. Marianne had cut horizontal lines to get the babies out, but Felix wasn't thinking about that, or about much of anything but getting rid of this treacherous whore. The more he hurt her, the more he hated her, and the more he wanted to hurt her. Her hands kept trying to interfere, trying to seize the knife, trying to bat him away, so he pulled out the blade and cut them, cut them so that with every move they flung blood somewhere, and Felix was covered with it. His cock, rock hard and bobbing over Trotski's naked body, shined with it.

He split her up to the place where he'd kissed her between the tits. She was still taking shallow breaths, but she didn't fight. Tears and snot covered her face, and her eyes bulged. None of that made Felix go limp. It was a *hate* hard-on.

The wide three-inch blade wasn't an ideal exploratory tool, but Felix used it to dig around until he felt confident that he was cutting into the uterus. What he was doing, what he had done, was a crime that carried the severest penalties—unless he could prove what he knew. If a time ever came for proving truth. Six out of nine True Sons, traitors. *Insurrection.*

When he'd cut a big enough hole, Felix stuck his right hand inside of Trotski, into blood and the clear goo that had erupted when he'd cut far enough into what he thought was the right place. He felt around until he believed he'd found it. Treating it with delicacy, he pulled the fetus out. He snapped the cord with his fingers.

The creature's head was almost the size of the entire rest of its body, which altogether wasn't much bigger than an avocado. He looked between its spindly legs. "I hope you like irony, Trotski.

Your journey didn't have to end for a long time." Unless he didn't know what he was seeing, the creature would have been a girl.

Holding the fetus in one hand, Felix crushed its head with his fingers and set it on Trotski's face. Trotski might have flinched, so he cut her throat. He set the knife aside and took his erection in his hand. Slowly, then faster as he glided along the fluids that had collected on his hand and his cock, he soothed the ache as he loomed over the ruined woman. He came in thunderbolts, shattering paroxysms, a deathly eruption of *not being*.

He returned to himself resolved. Six traitors. The night was young.

7. STALKER

His nose had been so overwhelmed by the acrid burning and rot with which Father's dissolving formula had tainted the air in the amphitheater—and then he'd been so distracted by other sensations—that he hadn't detected the air's most obvious warning: rain. His nostrils only registered the damp thickness after he'd left Trotski's corpse for someone to find and walked halfway to his training quarters, and by then drizzle had begun. As the precipitation picked up, he thought he might not need the shower he'd planned, but washing off the blood and gore and getting clean clothes to start anew sounded too good. He felt sticky, and sticky and stealthy seemed at odds. His private training quarters, a small building at the edge of the Settlement that he'd been granted once he'd been named, had shampoo and body wash and basic clothing and other supplies he wanted before he went hunting.

On a mission outside, a handgun with a silencer would be his weapon of choice, but using guns within the Lands was forbidden because guns cheapened death. In the decades of the Lands' existence, people had died by every other means imaginable, but not by gunshot. To transgress that taboo would be a silliness comparable to Salvador's. Felix would not use guns; he was better with other weapons anyway. After his shower he put on pants and a shirt that would cover his belt, which had loops for many knives. Some he chose because they were weighted for throwing, others because they had close combat advantages, and the bowie knife because it was badass. The blade on his main weapon wasn't quite twice the length of the bowie's blade. He chose a machete rather than a sword because he liked brute force and didn't know his way around a sword anyway. He felt fairly certain that the True Sons who carried swords didn't know how to wield them, either, but used them as patrician décor, which held no interest for Felix. For Felix, an axe would have been okay, but he found a machete more versatile. Cut, slice, slash, hack, chop. The machete had it all covered.

The uncountable, anonymous attendees at the wayward Sons' presentation had sparked a conundrum with their tragedy masks. Should he hide his identity? Wearing a comedy mask seemed appropriate, but he didn't know where to get one. The best he could do would be a hood or wrap. Anonymity would be a tactical advantage. But it didn't seem correct. He wouldn't eliminate himself by wearing a mask. That was only hiding. He would face the void naked, his willingness his abnegation. Let them know when the face death wore was his.

Eugene

Felix's belt didn't have a place for the machete, so when he went back into the rain, he carried it by his side. On his back he had his pack with only a few necessities, strapped closely to him to minimize noise. He didn't pass anyone on his return to Trotski's corpse. Under the cloud-dimmed night's dead stars and partial moon, the dead woman looked mostly as he'd left her, except her skin no longer glowed brown but had incongruous checkers of pale and dark like the mix of wet ashes around the burnt logs of the extinguished fire. The rain had washed a lot of blood away. The fetus with the crushed head still lay on her face.

With the machete's sharp tip, Felix brushed the fetus away. He raised the blade, aimed at the fissure he'd made when he'd slashed Trotski's throat, and whacked. No splatter. He whacked again. The head rolled away from the body. He picked up the head with its long black hair in his left hand and kept the machete, rinsing in rainwater, in his right. With the memory of Trotski leading him, he headed toward the amphitheater.

Enough time had passed for the place to have cleared out.

Alternately, six True Sons, six other young men with cultivated talents and tastes for providing death, could be on stage, and innumerable people could be in the audience. How many could Felix strike down before he succumbed? He imagined cutting through bodies like a field of grain, harvesting limbs, harvesting torsos, harvesting heads, hewing a corridor of blood through a waving, collapsing density.

He deviated from Trotski's path, approaching from the rear of the descending steps designed for seating. The stone tile-covered steps were abandoned, and all but two of the spotlights were off. The spots provided enough illumination on stage to show one person sitting at the center. The tub and chests were gone. Felix couldn't be certain no one else lurked in dark places, but he felt the naked man on the stage, Eugene, one of the oldest Sons, maybe second to Salvador, waited alone.

Stealth later: now, Felix descended the steps to the stage with only the rain to obscure him. At about halfway down, Eugene made eye contact with him, or at least came close by looking in the vicinity of his face, and called out: "Good evening, Felix!"

Felix noted the longsword lying flat across Eugene's lap. "Is it?" He continued his descent.

"I knew you'd be back," Eugene said, standing. With the tip on the stage, he balanced the sword handle with his right hand, but he didn't grip it. "What did you think about what you heard and saw?"

"It's not about all women," Felix said. He was close enough to the stage to feel like he was bowling as his left hand made the underhanded toss that landed Trotski's head near Eugene's sandaled feet.

Eugene looked down at the offering for a long moment while Felix stepped onto the stage and held at a gentlemanly distance. "I said," Eugene said, "be wary of the young ones. The ones most accustomed to Father. The ones who see him as... natural. Those of us who spent more time with the Father that was aren't as cowed by Father."

"Cowed?"

"Gill and Orion begged to differ, of course, and Puck was next to be invited, but Salvador wanted to tap you. 'Felix is smart,' he said. 'Felix questions things.' Answer me this: what difference does it make if we have another Father that was? It's all arbitrary. Father would admit that."

Felix eyed Eugene's right shoulder. Cutting off the sword arm would be a good message to start with. "And who would be realized as Father? You? Salvador?"

"A small Council with—"

Felix raised and lowered the machete like an axe aimed to split a log. He expected a single chop to pass through, parting arm from body, but instead—

CLANG!

Faster than his eyes could track, Eugene took a step and raised his sword at a strategic angle and with force that not only blocked Felix's downward swing but redirected its momentum so that Felix stumbled alongside his opponent, discombobulated and nearly disarmed.

The sword slashed across his back. It didn't disable him, but it stung. He felt his shirt blot the wet springing up around the diagonal cut.

Felix spun around and slapped away another incoming slash with a broad swing. Eugene centered the sword and aimed to split his skull, so Felix made another defensive swing, an arc in front of his face.

CLANG!

By the time Felix finished the arc, Eugene had recovered and jabbed at Felix's middle. The sword should have run him through, but instead—

clatter clatter clatter

Metal bounced on the stage. One of Felix's knives had fallen from his belt. The metal-covered belt not only blocked the sword, but it grabbed it. For an instant, Eugene couldn't pull back the blade, and an instant was all Felix needed.

The machete came down above the elbow of Eugene's right arm. Eugene staggered backward, screaming as his new stump sprayed blood in the spotlight. His forearm stayed with his hand, wrapped around the sword, held up where it stuck in Felix's belt. Felix dislodged the sword and kicked it away with Eugene's bleeding refuse.

The screaming. Eugene's screaming might wake up the whole Settlement. It might let the other five know he was coming.

Felix charged toward Eugene and chopped at his right leg below the knee. The machete gouged through muscle and bit into bone, but it didn't pass through. Felix chopped again, again, bits of skin and meat flying with blood as different chops created different wounds. The leg separated.

Instead of falling, Eugene lunged forward and latched his remaining hand onto Felix's right shoulder. Blood pouring from Eugene's stumps recolored Felix's fresh outfit while Eugene hopped, staying upright and leaning into Felix and pushing him, maybe even trying to topple him. Felix rammed the machete into Eugene's too-close gut and pushed his weapon's handle so Eugene would totter away.

Skewered on the machete, Eugene went backward but stayed upright. Felix gave the machete a quick thrust forward and quicker pull back, which made Eugene slide toward the tip of the blade, further away, but not all the way off the sharp bloody metal. Felix tried again, thrust and pull. After another shake, Eugene dropped from the blade's tip and looked down at the blood gushing in pulses from his middle. He looked back up at Felix with an unspecific question on his face.

Using all his strength, Felix took a wide, horizontal swing at Eugene's head. The machete made contact at mid-ear, passed through the skull, and exited through the ear on the other side. The top of Eugene's head flipped off and landed upside down on the stage. Felix supposed he was looking at two halves of a brain, which should have been interesting, but brain-halves looked a lot like other slop.

Eugene crumbled.

Benjy

Several of the True Sons adopted dogs as pets; Father had a dog. No amount of individual attention, however, could keep the dogs from acting as a pack, so most of the True Sons reasoned, with the support of the First House staff, that one Son could take charge of scheduled walks. Benjy, the biggest dog enthusiast of the bunch, stood out as the logical draftee, so he volunteered before anybody tried to twist his arm. He became the True Dogwalker.

Felix thought animal attachments were similar to human attachments and therefore distractions from the journey that made people brothers and sisters in the Lands, so he had nothing to do with canine goings-on and didn't pay attention to dog walking schedules but, as he approached First House from the rear through rain turning back into drizzle, recognized the bustle coming from the house's side as Benjy bringing the pooches for their goodnight pee. Convenient. Felix hid behind a trough full of flowers. In the garden behind First House, something always bloomed while something else died.

Benjy had a big contraption in his hand that made for a distracting puzzle until Felix figured out it contained at least five coils of leash, which would extend until the attached dog reached the limit, until Benjy pressed the stop button, or until Benjy pressed the button to make the coils retract. He'd seen retractable leashes designed for solitary dogs, but the group leash seemed clever for the True Dogwalker type. Benjy didn't talk much. Maybe he sat around inventing dogwalker tools all the time. Except when he played with the dogs. Felix didn't care.

The pack included two big dogs, one reddish and one beige, a lean medium-sized dog that looked like it could outrun a bullet train, and two small dogs, one that looked like a ball of white fluff and a yappy one that ran circles around other dogs when it got tired of simply running around in circles.
As the pack led Benjy closer to Felix's hiding spot, Felix thought he had to worry about the yappy dog, but the ball of fluff ran around the flower trough and rubbed against his feet and hindquarters as he crouched. It didn't bark, but the tiny bell on its collar dinged. The dinging fluffball.

Ding ding ding ding ding!

A quick poke with the bowie knife would end the problem.

He didn't want to kill it.

It licked his ankle. Fluff tickled his calf.

Ding ding ding ding ding!

"Yeti, where'd you go?" Benjy called. "Did you find something good?"

He did want to kill it. The problem was—

"Yeeeeeeeeeee-tiiiiiiiiiiiiiii!"

—he didn't know which dog belonged to Father. The dogs had to survive.

Woof! Woof! Woof!

One of the big dogs stood on the other side of the trough, undoubtedly barking at him. The bark wasn't hostile. No growling. These dogs knew Felix's scent. The dog barked as if to announce it had won the game of hide and seek. Benjy was close now, but a frontal attack, giving Benjy time to scream, wasn't wise beneath the windows of First House.

Giving "Yeti" a swift kick, which elicited a squeaky whine, Felix bolted along the trough. The big barking dog redoubled efforts as it sensed the movement, and Benjy said, "What is up with you guys tonight?" Benjy's voice let Felix know he'd gotten behind him, so he broke into the open and ran for cover behind a tree.

The big dog calmed. Mostly.

Woof!

Not entirely.

Benjy reasserted his status as alpha by retracting leashes and getting the pack in line before advancing further into the garden. Felix left his cover and crept on the toes of his sandals on a path behind Benjy and the dogs. The rain fell harder. Rainwater had diluted the blood in his clothes, spreading it through the fabric like a dye, making his outfit almost look like red was its intention, but not quite. If Benjy looked over his shoulder, or anyone glanced through one of First House's rear windows, what Felix was doing would be clear.

With the machine at shoulder height, Felix bounced from tiptoe to tiptoe, more in the air than on the ground. He got closer. The rain fell harder.

"All right, guys, we'd better get back inside. Hope you finished your business." Benjy turned around.

Leaping into the air, Felix swung the machete toward Benjy's neck.

Benjy looked startled before and after his head left his shoulders. The body fell belly-up behind the dogs, on top of their leash contraption, and the head flew away from the lamplit garden path.

Felix and the dogs gathered around the headless corpse, observing it curiously.

Felix remembered his tasting, the knowledge, the sensation, that bodies, empty embodiment, unified everyone in meaninglessness. Transgressing the body's alleged sacredness, not for political advancement like the traitors and their soup, but for its own sake—that was True. Father would be pleased.

Felix set aside the machete, took out one of his smaller knives, and cut a chunk from one of Benjy's shoulders. He held it up in front of the big reddish dog, which got the animal's attention. He waved it back and forth, then held it up in front of the dog's snout, making little jerks. Finally, the dog snapped it away from Felix's hand. With skillful chomps, the dog worked the skin and muscle into its mouth and shredded the tissues with its teeth.

A specially cut morsel got each of the other dogs involved. Then, Felix retrieved the machete. He hacked into Benjy, roughly separating meat from breastbones, arm bones, leg bones. He cut the meat into manageable chunks, making some extra small ones for Yeti and the yappy dog. Felix didn't know how much of Benjy these five well-fed dogs would eat, but they would get a good meal, and that seemed like enough.

Gill

Gill had a corner bedroom by the door to the True Sons' wing, so Felix could see where he slept near the center of his king-sized bed with only a sheet on top of him, the sheet pushed down to his waist, Gill peaceful and vulnerable in the dim light shining through the glass, unsuspecting. Eugene had suspected. Were the rest of them morons?

Felix stripped in the rain, letting the quickening waterfall wash the stickiness from his skin before he put the belt back on, leaving the reddened clothes to soak on the dirt trail. He knew what he was going to do. In his mind, he was already crawling across the king-sized bed.

When he did crawl, Gill turned in his direction, but he didn't open his eyes. He made a satisfied "Mmm." Felix imagined him dreaming of food. Gill was the pudgiest of the Sons. Beneath the pudge he was solid muscle, seldom outmatched in friendly wrestling bouts, but he had chubby cheeks and some blubber around the middle. He had once confided in Felix that one of the greatest advantages of being a True Son was having unlimited access to cheese. Felix had never comprehended the connection between cheese and death, but he supposed it had something to do with mold.

The backpack had stayed by Gill's bedroom door along with the machete. From the pack Felix had taken the duct tape, now hanging from the belt, which had everything else he needed. The ripping plastic noise of peeling and cutting the tape to cover Gill's mouth made Gill's eyes open and his head turn to face upward—perfect—so on a downward dive Felix fastened the strip of silver and made Gill start to buck.

Felix put his weight on Gill's upper body while pulling up the sheet. He rolled and worked while Gill squirmed beneath him. Throwing knives from his belt became pins, sticking the white fabric to the mattress above Gill's arms, by Gill's sides, beside Gill's legs. He moved like an overturned beetle, scampering for connection with a surface that refused him, repelled him, encased him. Beneath the tape, he made useless sounds.

Beneath the sheet, he reached for Felix, which wasn't quite as useless.

However, Felix had the bowie knife, and its use came after the pinning knives. Through the white sheet he stabbed into the grabbing hand, piercing the palm from behind, tip of the blade perforating the mattress. The knife came back with airborne red, and the hand left an expanding trail of red in the white as it retreated, and Felix wondered about so much white fabric in the Settlement, asking for blood.

As one of Gill's legs kicked up under the sheet, Felix stabbed it. The other kicked up, and he stabbed that, too. The thighs shifted from one side to the other, as if he might break through a barrier pin and roll away, so Felix stabbed at them, sure he was cutting into quadriceps on the tops and the sides, but all he saw were the red blossoms on the white covering, wet but he was already wet, cleaner than he'd been but covered with rainwater, so he felt glad the sheet controlled most of the splatter. An arm tried to reach up out of the sheet, and it got stabbed.

Finally, Gill sat up partway, pushing with bleeding hands and arms against the sheet, disconnecting the knives at his shoulders from the mattress, flexing his solid stomach. Felix stabbed through the flab, into the rigid abs, and Gill froze. A second stab made Gill fall back on the bed, and then the arms and legs stopped their beetle impression. The scrambling at an unhelpful, now quite red, sheet stopped. Gill's eyes remained wide, and they fixed on Felix.

Felix frenzied: more stabs in the stomach, four, five, ten, in between ribs, and into the chest, more into what remained of the meat of the arms and legs, the sheet shredded, the splatter uncontrolled. His own skin was red again, and he thought about going back in the rain. He wouldn't, though. He'd look like a nightmare when he came for Orion, Mister, and Salvador. He *was* a nightmare.

The killing was purifying him. He felt it. Giving death brought him closer to the void. He was its ally tonight. After Father, he might be the second closest thing to divinity in the

Lands and under the dead stars.

He was realized as justice, punishment, and wrath.

Orion

Orion, who'd once ripped off a man's face with his bare hands, was afraid of him. Afraid of Felix, but also, and more importantly, afraid of Felix as a vessel of Father, because once Felix *called* himself Father's vengeance, Orion's fight left him. "Okay, okay. What do I do? What... penance... does Father demand?"

If Felix claimed to know whether Father would consider penance, he'd be lying. All his actions stemmed from Father's suspicion and a comment that if his suspicion turned out to be correct, they would have to resort to extreme measures. The remainder of the day, and the night, had come from Felix's intuition and initiative. But confidence flowed through him. What kind of penance did Father demand?

One idea led to another. *Pinning.* Felix told Orion to sit at the wooden table where he took his meals when he didn't want to socialize in the common area. As Orion complied, Felix asked where he kept his tools. Orion indicated a cabinet where Felix found a toolbox with an appropriate hammer and, beside it, a box of sufficient nails. He brought the supplies to the table and said, "You're a lefty, aren't you?"

Orion nodded. He also looked thin. Didn't exercise as much as the others.

Felix said, "Stick out your arms, flatten your right hand, palm down, on the table, and spread out your fingers." Felix set the hammer and nails on the table so that Orion knew what was coming. He hesitated but did as he was told.

Felix held the nail in position over the tip of Orion's pinky. He set the hammer near Orion's left hand. "Drive it through."

"I...." He picked up the hammer and weighed it while he stared at his splayed hand. "What if I can't?"

"You'll do that and more."

Hesitation. Felix gave the machete a playful wave through

the air. Hesitation.

"Remember not to scream," Felix said.

Orion raised the hammer.

Felix didn't expect him to do it, but the hammer came down, an exact strike, and the point of the iron nail sank down through the fingernail in a bright red squirt. Orion heaved an inward rush of air to stifle the scream that wanted to escape, and he hit the nail's head again and again. The fingertip split, but he kept going until the nail held its two sides firmly against the table's wood.

Orion wept, stared at his ruined pinky, and struggled to control his breathing. "F-f-f-father...."

"Yes, Father," Felix said. He set up the nail on the next finger.

Hesitation.

WHAM! WHAM! WHAM!

In addition to the five fingers, they drove five nails into the center of the hand. They had a trail going halfway up the arm before Orion said, with a lot of interruptions from faltering breath, "You're going to kill me anyway."

Another decapitation.

Mister

Blood-drenched, wearing only the belt and the backpack, carrying the machete in his right hand and the bowie knife in his left, dripping, an extended stain as he moved down the stately hall, Felix arrived at Mister's door before the full significance of Orion's surrender struck him.

Orion never screamed. He didn't scream because he thought he owed Father his quiet compliance. Father's power, Father's charm, reasserted itself as the traitor got closer to death. Father was life, and Father was death.

Felix didn't know whether he'd have the self-control not to scream as nails pierced his fingertips and shattered the brittle bones of his hand. None of his experiences led him to believe he had special resistance to pain.

Mister could scream. All First House could awaken now. Felix had begun to restore order, but the greater exigencies of the Settlement needed prompt consideration.

The door wasn't locked. Felix went through, into the dark room, closed the door behind him, passed the bathroom, moved toward the mass on one side of the king-sized bed—and felt the knife at his throat.

"Do I kill you, do you kill me, or do I kill myself?" Mister asked. The blade, ordinary for hunting, maybe four inches, pressed against Felix's skin, so Felix didn't turn to look at Mister or move his jaw to answer. "We could both kill ourselves." Mister jerked the knife away and pushed Felix farther into the room. He punched a button on the wall. Bright light filled the space. Felix in the main room, Mister in the entryway, they were two strong young men who had killed before and who held blades they could kill with now. They eyed one another. Neither showed eagerness. "I couldn't sleep. I figured you'd come. If not you, somebody."

"Drop the knife, and I'll make it quick," Felix said. He hardly knew Mister, and Mister hadn't killed him when he could have.

"Do you have two minds, Felix?" Mister held on to the knife, but his stance was infirm. "One mind sees life as the great journey to the void, the shedding of self until the great moment when you embrace death, and that's the *right* mind, the *good* mind, but the other... has desires... to live... and knows everything about what we do here is either bullshit or madness."

Mister cringed as if he expected an immediate thrashing from the machete, but Felix only studied him while he considered an answer other than "yes." Two minds. Father wasn't a god. He said so himself. He was the adhesive on duct tape. Cohesion, coherence: his bullshit bound the community in their rituals, ways of living and dying, and fulfilled them, so what might be madness from an outside perspective was a higher sanity. Death was universal and inevitable. Clinging to the fear of it seemed like madness. Father stood for a greater truth, a greater sanity that married divided minds. "The second mind," Felix said, "is the impurity we work so hard to cleanse."

"I know. I knew it tonight, at the amphitheater. Salvador... Salvador thinks that because Father replaced the Father that was, someone else can replace Father as easily." Mister lowered his arm but didn't drop the knife. "But on that stage tonight...."

"Salvador isn't Father," Felix said.

"Some of us falling in with him have talked about a Council leadership, but—"

"That's the kind of bullshit that won't work. Not here."

"Will you help me?" Mister asked. "I need abnegation. Abasement before I end my journey. Purification."

"Lie on your back," Felix said. "On the edge of the bed."

Mister dropped his knife and walked close to the machete to get to the bed, where he stretched out as expected on an edge with plenty of room to maneuver beside it. Before he followed, Felix picked up Mister's knife. He set it on a nightstand Mister could reach.

He'd gotten Orion to drive nails through his hand. What could he get Mister to do?

What might be most difficult *not* to fight against?

Felix set the machete aside and took an average-length but *sharp* knife from his belt. "You can scream," he said, "but don't fight. It's the self that fights."

Mister nodded. His limbs trembled. Felix remembered reading a sermon called "Sinners in the Hands of an Angry God" when he was in school. Fucked up religion, that was. All that fear of torture at the hands of a heavenly Father, no hope of oblivion. Mister trembled like one of those sinners.

Orion's fear had been miraculous. And Orion hadn't *asked* for abnegation.

With his left hand, Felix cupped Mister's genitals, scrotum and penis. He gathered and lifted them away from the cleft of his thighs. The penis stirred, grateful for stimulation despite the fear pumping adrenaline to Mister's flexing extremities.

Felix slipped the blade beneath the scrotum, where he imagined the metal, slick with rainwater, felt cold.

"Gaaaaah," Mister said.

"Ready?" Felix smiled and leaned in to catch Mister's eyes.

Mister blinked.

Felix forced the blade into flesh, pushing in tip to handle, tip to handle, seesawing, making a wide, slender tunnel beneath Mister's balls and through the base of his cock. Mister shrieked, and his limbs alternately jumped without rhythm from the mattress, but he didn't fight. Thick blood covered both of Felix's hands as he worked body in the left and blade in the right, and Mister made sounds like, "GAH-huh, GAH-huh, GAH-huh," his pitch rising and falling but not soaring into soprano. The knife reached a place where it didn't want to go any further, so Felix changed sides, starting in at the top of the penis and aiming downward as if to connect with the tunnel he was making from the other side. The visible part of the penis fell off before he connected, but he did connect, and the hidden root, tissues and tubes and veins and arteries, along with the scrotum, testicles untucked, came loose. Felix tossed the bloody mass to the unoccupied side of the bed.

"GAH-huh, GAH-huh, GAH-huh!"

"You want to finish it?"

Mister, blood spreading around his middle, tears gleaming against a greenish complexion, nodded with vigor while the agonized noises kept erupting from his mouth.

Felix picked up Mister's knife from the nightstand and put it in Mister's right hand. Fingers closed around the handle, but the hand didn't rise. Felix lifted both hands and joined them in the air above Mister's chest, where fingers laced around the handle, blade pointed down.

Felix stepped back. For a few seconds, he thought Mister might not do anything. Then, the knife blade arced into Mister's stomach. Mister's arms tensed as he pulled the blade through his belly toward his sternum, where he gave it one last jerk before he stopped moving.

Watching Mister go to the void, Felix felt good about what he'd done.

8. SALVADOR

"Death requires living. That... simple truth always gave you trouble. You accept everything else Father says. How do you embrace the journey toward death without a lust for the living that gets you there?"

Salvador sat sideways in the big chair at the divider that separated the back half of First House's wide central hall from the front half, where Father received petitions from the Settlement's ordinary brothers and sisters. The chair Salvador occupied, his bare back against one of the chair's arms, his bare legs draped over the other, his white shorts on the red cushion, was for Father when he led meetings with the True Sons. Salvador sat improperly in an improper place, a deliberate spectacle, a taunting usurpation. He posed for Felix, who faced him as he walked from the end of the Sons' wing to the center of the hall, machete tapping on air, blood from recent encounters tickling him as it crawled downward over most of his exposed skin. "I have appetites," Felix said. "I'm not yet done living."

Dark curly hair, puffy lips, body like a figment from classical sculpture, Salvador looked at the ceiling as he chuckled, and Felix glimpsed why Salvador was *something else* to Father. The brown-skinned seraph said, "Have you considered living *well*?"

"I concentrate on dying well." If Felix brought the machete down in a straight line toward the center of the chair, he might cut Salvador neatly in halves. Did that seem right?

"Do you like living in First House?" Salvador faked *sang froid.*

Felix said, "It's an honor."

"It's pretty comfortable, too, don't you think? Nice rooms,

great food… a lot better than what you knew growing up."

Honors came with perks. "Okay. And?"

"We make a point of communal living that's superior to outside, but it's all rather medieval, isn't it? Living in the shadow of the Father-King's castle?"

Felix stepped close, machete tapping on empty air. "That's ridiculous."

Salvador swung his legs toward the floor, straightened his posture, and reached down beside the chair, where he picked up a weapon—a shotgun, double-barreled—that Felix hadn't noticed. "I could put a big hole in you, turn that young body of yours into chunks and spray." He laughed. "But hold still for the moment."

Felix held still. The machete stopped tapping.

"You know how much the outside revolves around *money*," Salvador said. "We supposedly have little use for it. We look down on them for it."

Father provides. Father is life. Father is death.

"Do you know how much *money* Father has? Or could have?"

If Felix ran toward him, could he attack before Salvador pulled the trigger? Could they go down together?

He wasn't close enough. "Father provides all we need," Felix said.

"Every time he wants another hundred million or so, he sells another patent for one of his chemical concoctions," Felix said. "Or the concoctions from the Father that was. He's sitting on billions and billions of dollars' worth of intellectual property. Every brother and sister in the Settlement could live like a king or queen."

Felix recalled the elaborate clothing and sparkling jewelry he'd seen outside, the contrast between the wealthier and the poorer areas, and his stomach turned. "Luxury distracts from the journey."

"Does it?" Salvador stood, shotgun pointed at Felix. "Who's to say we shouldn't wallow in luxury until we've had our fill, *then* meet the void? Who's to say that's not the best preparation?"

"Father," Felix said.

"Father is only a man," Salvador said. "What if he's wrong?"

"Right and wrong don't matter," Felix said. He smiled. "Father is Father."

"I knew talking to you would be a waste, but I did hope." Salvador aimed the shotgun, finger on the trigger. "Goodbye, Felix."

Piw!

A dart hit Salvador's neck, and one of his hands left the shotgun to slap at it like a mosquito. A second later, he dropped to his knees, then crashed forward, shotgun clattering beside him.

Felix turned. Behind him, Father lowered a rifle that looked like his own. "It was a low dose," Father said. "I'll help you with him."

*

He'd never imagined what Father's private room for sacrifices in First House would look like, but when Father led him in, the two of them carrying Salvador, Felix absorbed the surroundings and decided they were what he would have imagined. Along the wall opposite the door in the squarish chamber, simple wooden chairs formed a line as if on the dais. Although one chair had the center space and thus must have belonged to Father, it blended in the way Father blended, whereas the more ostentatious chair where Felix had found Salvador seemed like a relic of the Father that was.

The combination of the chairs with horrific practicality sparked instant fondness for the room. Along the other walls, doorless cabinets, finer furniture than the chairs, displayed weaponry, much of it with a medieval quality, arranged in categories, swords and related blades, axes, polearms, spears, maces, morningstars, flails, various vises and specialized devices for crushing and spreading and splitting and twisting bones and joints and ligaments and muscles and skin, all the hard parts, all the soft parts, torture made easy by finely tuned technologies.

They dropped Salvador at the room's center, in an empty space around which structures, bolted to the stone floor, seemed designed to hold people in various awkward positions. Felix recognized one structure as more or less a pillory, but it was unusual because it was too high for most adults to kneel and too low for most adults to stand, an optimal height for discomfort, an ingenious upgrade. The other shapes with fastenings seemed related in torturous purpose, but Felix would have to experiment with them to understand them.

"You've done so much," Father said. Felix assumed Father knew about all his night's activities. "I hate to ask you to… finish the matter… with Salvador."

"You don't have to ask," Felix said. He regretted the sadness in Father's eyes. He resented Salvador.

Father sat in his chair.

Despite the inherent intrigue of the perverse arsenal along the walls and the contortion-inducing structures on the floor, the bars near the ceiling, bars with hooks for attachments, established the decisive grip on his imagination. On the floor, Salvador twitched. A shoulder jumped toward his ear. His head turned. Felix didn't have much time.

In one of the least conspicuous cabinets in one of the room's back corners, Felix found the first thing he needed: rope.

With the polearms, he found the second: a plain metal pole.

Salvador's right leg jerked, a reflex, a startle response as he faded into consciousness, when Felix wrapped and tied the rope around his ankle. A murmur. Salvador murmured.

Felix focused. Gaining momentum on a count of three, he tossed the coil of rope at one of the hooks curving downward from a bar near the ceiling's center. He missed.

Father watched.

Felix gathered the rope and tried again. One, two, three— throw!

Salvador whispered, moaned, "Sebastian."

The hook caught the rope. Felix straightened out the side of the rope that fell back down. He pulled it taut and heaved, lifting

Salvador's bare leg and covered middle into the air.

"Why?" Salvador was more audible.

Felix heaved again, lifting Salvador into the air.

"What's happening?" Salvador flapped on the end of the rope, making it harder to hold.

Sweat formed on Felix's brow, back, chest, and arms, and the moisture gathered and dripped, making the blood spatter all over his skin stickier. He pulled the rope once, twice, lifting Salvador higher and higher as the young man's body became more animated. A third pull got the waking body high enough. Quickly, before his strength gave out, Felix rushed to one of the body-contorting structures and tied the rope around it, securing Salvador where he dangled, flapped, and swung.

"FELIX!" Salvador yelled, his head turning so that, when he swayed in the right direction, the two "True" Sons could see one another, though each saw the other upside down and swinging like a wild pendulum.

As Felix retrieved the pole he'd selected, he thought of all the medieval weaponry, thought of talking about the Inquisition in school, and thought of a clever way to proceed. "Salvador," he said, "it's time for you to confess." Felix stood close to the man whose face was already bulging with the blood rushing to his head, silently daring him to try using the low-hanging hands Felix had deliberately left free.

Salvador was groggy. "He... he's making you do his dirty work."

"I volunteered." After the business with the rope, the long metal pole seemed heavy, but Felix could handle it. Salvador tried to control the way the rope swung, but he couldn't stop the collision of his bare left side with Felix's metal.

CRACK!

Salvador howled as the area beneath his armpit caved in, changing from its golden tan to purple, red, and black. The rope swung faster. Father watched.

"Kill me then!" Salvador demanded.

"Confess!" Felix prepared the metal pole. The next strike

required control and accuracy. Hitting the head now, so soon, would be a mistake. Father watched with a glint in his eye.

Salvador saw the strike coming and held his left arm up to cover the dent in his side. Felix's aim was lower, though, beneath the head, on a level with the right arm, which swung with the pull of gravity, reaching limply for the floor until—

SNAP!

The pole hit the upper arm, and Felix would have sworn he felt the vibration of the humerus as it broke in two. The arm wobbled limply, out of sync with the flapping, swaying body, while Salvador screamed. His left arm grabbed at his right arm as if it might start moving with a push.

"Confess!"

"WHAT DO I CONFESS?"

"Admit your wrongs to Father!"

"HE KNOWS ALREADY!"

Felix prepared a strike, aiming higher, but first he raised his volume: "CONFESS!"

Salvador's head jerked back and forth. Instead of trying to look at Felix, he tried to look at Father. "I tried to start a rebellion." His voice cracked with stress and sustained volume. "We could have killed you. We would have." Salvador swung, back, forth, back, forth.

Metal smashed into Salvador's bare stomach. His left leg, so far bent toward the suspended right one, kicked at the air, and his bashed torso curled for an instant before his body stretched out, face swollen, burgundy. His mouth opened and released choking sounds, followed by coughs that ejected blood and unidentifiable, blood-soaked solids. Trickles continued from Salvador's lips down his cheeks to his forehead. He moaned and wiggled while he swung.

"Confess," Felix said. He readied a strike.

"I confessed." Salvador didn't try to yell, but he made himself heard. "Why do this, Felix? You don't... you can't be... this isn't... you don't..." he coughed, spewing blood, *"like it."*

A True Son cultivates sadism.

The pole hit the free leg as it kicked empty air. No satisfying crack, but the leg bent in an odd direction, and Salvador grunted. Maybe he couldn't scream.

As Salvador swung near, Felix grabbed him by the neck, and Salvador's momentum almost lifted him from the floor. Felix stopped the pendulum, though; he held Salvador still. Felix whispered in Salvador's ear, "Purge your *self* before you greet the void. Seek purification. Who... and *what*... did you betray?"

Felix stepped back and readied the metal pole.

"You're crazy," Salvador said.

"Confess."

Salvador tried to turn toward the chairs but couldn't. "I betrayed Father!"

The pole struck the suspended right leg.

CRACK!

The thigh bent as the pendulum regained motion. A high-pitched screech left Salvador's mouth along with jets of fluid from his damaged organs. The dark red of his face's swelling was becoming difficult to see beneath the lighter red of the blood spilling from his mouth.

Felix spun around and struck again, hitting the loose right arm. The metal struck the forearm with a weak *crack*, but the upper arm showed the damage as skin tore, bone poked through, and what might have been a strand of muscle flopped out. Salvador struggled to control his breathing.

"What did you betray!" Felix demanded.

"Everything! Life! Death! Everything!"

"Purge your *self*!" Smiling, no longer noticing the pole's weight, Felix swung at the swinging man and connected with his back, spreading discoloration, making Salvador's breathing more erratic.

"I, I, I—"

"WHAT DID YOU DO?" Felix yelled as he struck both legs, knocking the left leg into an independent spiral, making the right thigh's unnatural bend sharper. Salvador convulsed.

"Kill m—"

"CONFESS!"

"I betrayed the Settlement of Passing!"

"Worse!"

"I betrayed our beliefs!"

Felix struck the loose right arm. The metal pole didn't stop when it hit. It disconnected the arm beneath the shoulder and carried the limb through the rest of its path. The arm sprayed blood in a wider arc as it rode with the pole, then fell to the floor as Felix's weapon halted. Salvador's bleeding was profuse, flooding the stone floor. He wouldn't last much longer.

Father watched. Felix couldn't interpret his expression.

On a surge of anger, Felix said, "What did you have that made you feel special, special enough to lead an insurrection? What did you have that was yours alone that you betrayed? Purge your *self*."

"I... I...."

Felix waved the metal pole in the air.

"I had...."

Felix aimed at the suspended leg, the unnaturally bent thigh.

Salvador finished, "I had Father's love."

Repeatedly, as hard and fast as he could, Felix struck Salvador's suspended leg. It changed colors. Skin broke and bled. Deeper tissues, the thin fatty layer, the thicker muscle, mashed and split. Bone cracked, snapped, broke in two, became visible. The pole beat its way through the leg, helped by the pendulum effect's added force.

Salvador landed in blood on the stone floor, the bottom part of his right leg dangling above him. He wheezed.

Felix used the metal pole like a long hammer, beating at Salvador's crumpled body, no longer aiming. The pile of man became a pile of purple and red. Black hair stripped from the scalp that tore free when the skull finally crunched peppered the mix of skin, muscle, and bone. The insides blended with the outsides, adding more pinks and blues. The smell wasn't like ripping out Hugo's intestines. He couldn't really describe it to himself. When nothing recognizable remained of Salvador, he dropped the pole and felt the beginning of his muscles' ache. He'd stopped noticing the moisture on his skin at some point, but it came back with vengeance, drenching him. No part of his naked body felt free of a soup of sweat, blood, and pulverized human remains.

Father was smiling. Felix was pleased.

9. THE FACELESS

The rain had stopped, and the clouds had cleared. Felix had clean skin and clothes.

Once in a while, the brothers and sisters debated pouring concrete and laying brick on the main streets of the Settlement, but they didn't have cars or other wheeled transportation, so no one ever invested the effort, and, as mud sucked at his sandals, Felix wished they'd felt motivated to do *that*.

The brothers and sisters.

When Felix had told Father about the audience in masks, the frowning mass, Father had sighed without seeming crestfallen. He'd suspected. He talked about sensing *blight*. Smelling decay.

Remove the rot. But how far did it reach?

Salvador must have had more activity planned for this long, long night. Felix walked the Settlement's streets and observed the shuttered windows of the linked dwellings. Not all the doors, but many of them displayed the white ceramic tragedy masks Salvador's audience, Salvador's followers, had worn. Signs. Identifiers. Statements of allegiance.

So many doors. Felix couldn't knock on them all.

He chose one at random.

The woman who answered wore a white smock that draped smoothly over the bulge in her middle, down to her knees, and she had her hair tied in a long dark ponytail that arched above her left ear. She blinked at him with curled eyelashes and didn't look like a traitor.

Approaching behind her, a thin, fair young woman said, "Who is it?"

The woman in the doorway surprised Felix when she said, "One of the True Sons. The new one."

The woman who didn't look pregnant, who wore a tunic and pants a lot like Felix's, got close to the bigger woman's side but hung back in the narrow foyer. "Is he—"

"He hasn't said anything yet."

"My name is Felix," he said.

"Okay." The woman in the smock glanced at the woman in pants, who shrugged, then said, "What can we help you with, Felix?"

He hadn't thought that far ahead. The desire to know what the masks on the door meant combined with the urge to end the blight to make him want to make contact with—they'd stopped being brothers and sisters, hadn't they, and become the enemy? Contact with the enemy. But what to do with the contact now that he'd secured it... "I just spoke with Salvador," he said. "He sent me out to learn." He thought of commenting on them being awake and dressed at this hour, but he said, "May I enter?"

Again, the obviously pregnant woman looked to the other, whose fear-widened eyes didn't blink as she gave a slight nod that seemed more question than answer. "Of course," the woman in the doorway said, and she backed up, gesturing toward the warmly lit living room that closed shutters kept invisible to the outside.

After Felix stepped inside and passed the thin woman, the rounder woman closed the door, and he heard her throw the latch. People didn't lock their doors in the Settlement of Passing. They had no crime because brothers and sisters could satisfy criminal urges outside and because satisfying them inside would rush you unpleasantly to the void. The brothers and sisters lived plainly, as extravagance was not conducive to self-abnegation, but anything they truly wanted, Father could and would provide. They had no reasonable motive for distrust. For rebellion.

These two women looked like fine sisters. But something was wrong with them.

They were insane.

"Would you like to sit down? I could put on tea," the

obviously pregnant woman said.

Could he trust tea from her? Why did she lock the door?

He had the bowie knife strapped to his thigh and several smaller knives on the belt that his tunic covered. But this was *their* house. The sofa cushions, the rug, the bookshelves—weapons and traps could be anywhere. Salvador had known he was coming. Had Salvador sent out a message before—?

Felix sat on the sofa and said, "Nothing for me, thanks. I won't take much of your time."

The two women didn't sit on the loveseat or chairs. They stood together, nearby. "We've been waiting for the message," one of them said.

What if they were both pregnant? How many people were in the room? Felix didn't know which way he wanted the numbers to go. The way they'd kept standing had caught him off guard. They had a tactical and psychological advantage. If they had weapons. If they knew to be at war.

"I'm afraid I don't know much. Salvador didn't clue me in until tonight, and there's been trouble since the meeting at the amphitheater. Orion's trying to confirm, but we think Father knows. The other True Sons are working on a new plan."

The women gasped. "Father knows! What will happen to us?"

"That's what we're trying to figure out, and I've got catching up to do," Felix said. "Tell me, what message were you *hoping* to get?"

"That we were selected as part of the New Fold, and the location of our new meeting place." The women looked scared, uncertain.

"Do you know if the message was to be written?" Felix asked. Did these women actually have information he wanted? He knew what he wanted to *do*. But to know? The term "New Fold" infuriated him with its mock authenticity.

Thin and round looked at one another. One shrugged, and the other said, "We don't—know—why is it—"

"I think Salvador was smart enough not to write it down.

For your sake, I hope so. Otherwise, your journeys... well, unless you think...." He knew what he wanted to know. It was a lesser wanting.

"Think what?"

"How many," he said. So many frowning white masks on doors. So many journeys to end. "Do enough brothers and sisters agree with Salvador for us to overcome Father and his supporters?"

"Over half the Settlement." The pronouncement didn't make the woman sound any less afraid.

"Thank you," Felix said. He stood, stretching his arms.

The women stepped back.

Shoving his hand down his pants to pull out the bowie knife lacked grace, but he didn't lack speed. The obviously pregnant one broke toward the kitchen, but she only took two long leaps before he blocked her and swung his blade at her throat. He didn't sever the head, which was disappointing, but he did cleave neck-flesh in a fine spray. Wetness combined with the sound of the body falling behind him as he turned to catch up with the thin woman in pants, who'd run in the opposite direction, toward the front door.

Felix laughed. The lock flummoxed her, stopped her long enough for him to reach her.

He returned the bloody bowie to its place on his thigh, and, directly behind her, boxed her in with the foyer's walls at her sides and the locked door in front of her. He grabbed her shoulders.

She shrieked.

He threw her against the left wall, and the rough collision knocked the scream out of her. Allowing no time for recovery, he grabbed her and slammed her against the door, then flung her to the wall on the right, which she hit with a satisfying *crack*.

What had she hoped to gain?

A tug at her limp arm spun her so he could shove her against the opposite wall. After she hit it, he shifted closer, gripped the back of her head, and smashed her face against the vertical surface. He didn't stop when pulling her head back and forth made trails of bloody snot between her broken nose and shattered mouth and the wall. Bits of teeth fell on the wood-tiled floor.

Felix threw her face-down on the tiles and listened to her moan. The women hadn't been prepared, or if they'd prepared, they'd failed to act. They'd lacked *motivation*. They disappointed him at every level. They weren't sisters. They were trash.

He stomped on her back. *CRACK!*

"Oooooh—"

She wasn't very loud now. That first shriek, though. The neighbors had to have heard.

Would they dare show themselves?

Felix jumped on her back. The snaps and cracks were many. Her sound was small even as, or maybe because, her ribcage collapsed.

Blood made her right pants leg cling to her thigh. He hadn't done anything to make that happen, had he? Or maybe she'd been pregnant after all.

He stomped on her head. Muddy sandals weren't good for crushing skulls, but eventually, he managed.

A True Son cultivates sadism. His exhilaration was his cultivation, movement toward purification.

He imagined going house to house, stomping the life out of every traitor. It wouldn't work—the brothers and sisters would catch on, overpower him—and he didn't have time, anyway. But he had an idea, and he thought he had an ally.

And he would have more to report to Father than the excision of two women before asking him to do his part in removing the rot.

*

Kate, who stood at the edge of the dirt circle wearing a leather mask and wielding a whip to make sure contestants didn't violate the strictures, lived in the teachers' quarters attached to the nursery, where fewer than half the teachers chose to live—but she was devoted. Reliable, hence her honored role as Monitor, a secret everyone knew. Another open secret: she had the privilege of being barren, having had a medically necessary hysterectomy at nineteen, years before Father discovered her. She knew many things, and she would not be disloyal.

Hearing of the insurrection, she merely asked, "What would Father want of me?"

"Assemble the other teachers," Felix said.

Summoned from their quarters or less monkish Settlement locales, the teachers gathered in the school's main hall, some of them obviously confused from having been dragged from their beds, wanting to know if the fuss was tied to the order to keep their shutters closed, some of them more alert, suspiciously alert. Felix's observations of alertness had a high correlation with Kate's choices when she separated the nervous, jabbering mass into a group of people she deemed trustworthy and a group she did not, a separation the nature of which they kept secret from the nervous educators. The wakeful ones, however, seemed to recognize each other, and they seemed to sense the void's approach.

They talked less than the other group. When Felix told the other group to fetch chairs from the dining hall, the untrustworthy ones became somber.

Several of them looked at Felix. If they were smart, they were sizing him up, wondering if they could take him on, calculating whether they could get away from him. If one of them could lead, organize, Felix and Kate wouldn't stand a chance, even though at some point she'd picked up a hammer she looked too small to lift. The teachers who'd decided to rebel couldn't be *completely* stupid. They might have been insane like those two pregnant women, but they weren't stupid. Fear overruled intelligence. They feared Father, and Felix represented him. Transmitted him.

Felix brought his justice.

He whispered in Kate's ear, and she said she'd be right back with what he wanted. With the help of the trustworthy group —the others looking on, not knowing what was happening but knowing it couldn't be good for them—Felix arranged the chairs into two rows, facing each other.

He told the untrustworthy group to take off their clothes, and a man—the teachers were mostly men—rushed at him, yelling some incoherent battle cry. The man was fast, but Felix got a knife from his belt faster and jammed it into the man's eye. The man froze, arms and legs positioned as if he might run farther forward at any moment, until Felix dislodged the modest blade, a squirt of reddish yellow trailing it. The man's head turned toward the group from which he'd sprung, astonishment everywhere on his face but his leaking, punctured, bulging eye, then collapsed.

Grumbles. The group disrobed.

No one seemed surprised when Felix told the naked group to fill the chairs, and all were quiet once they settled, naked and facing each other. No one was humiliated or self-conscious even though the teachers had some of the Settlement's older and less attractive bodies, but the seated ones looked uniformly scared. They knew death was coming, but they didn't know how or when. The members of the trustworthy group also looked uncomfortable. They knew death was coming for their colleagues, but they didn't know why.

Too much concern for knowing.

When Kate came back into the hall and walked along one row, handing each teacher a steak knife, tension tightened. Those who received knives didn't look happy to have them. Those who didn't clearly wanted them.

Felix readied his bowie knife, and Kate, knives distributed, held her hammer in two hands. "Disloyalty asserts the self before belief," Felix said, looking at the teachers in the chairs, looking at the floor between them. "It is ugly and doesn't belong here. Some of you have put too much faith in your own judgment, so I am testing that faith. Those of you on this side," he gestured to the row with the knives, "have knives in your hands and unarmed people across from you. Exercise your judgment. Use the knife on yourself—quite noble!—or dispatch the person you're facing. As for those of you on this side," and he gestured to the row of people understanding they'd been made targets, "whether you let them exercise their judgment is up to you."

"You all betrayed Father!" Kate yelled.

The trustworthy group, not needing her instigation, had already spread through the hall, blocking exits. The teachers looked at each other, searched the room. Felix felt certain they considered fighting, fleeing, everything but Felix's test of their faith, and their faces said *impossible, impossible, impossible.* Why? Felix sensed what they were about to do, and he felt awe.

Charismatic.

He channeled Father, and Father shaped their vision, making them see only the options Felix provided, killing themselves and killing each other.

The traitors put too much value on life. Hope for survival would taint their judgment. Those with knives would choose to use them. Those without knives would die trying to get them. The school's main hall was about to host an implosion of insurrectionists.

"If you come to me with a knife in one hand," Felix said, "and a severed head in the other, I will let you live." He paused. "Father will let you live."

A brief pause, and then a man in the knife row made a cry like the man who had rushed at Felix, only he hurled himself across the aisle toward the row of chairs filled with the unarmed, toward another man who was only halfway standing by the time his attacker arrived. The attacker raised the knife overhead and brought it down in an arc, drove the blade in between shoulder and neck, used his other hand to push his quarry back down in his chair, and descended, plunging the knife into flesh from every angle his hand could find, splashing blood on people around him, spilling it on the floor—

and people around him got out of their chairs, backed away, looked toward their counterparts with knives, crinkled their faces, became more animal—

and another man, and a woman, both with knives, crossed the aisle, attacking counterparts more ready to defend themselves

—the woman tried to stab a man's neck, but the man grabbed her arm, twisted it, made her drop her weapon—

which the man next to him picked up and used to stab him, not her. She ducked away as the man she'd been after, stunned, got stabbed in the chest, then the face, by the man he'd been sitting by.

Weapons changed hands. Knives stabbed into thighs, sliced open bellies, carved valleys wherever metal reached flesh. A man slipped on the blood accumulating on the floor, fell, conked his head, didn't seem out—

except he got trampled by two people, both with knives, making desperate jabs while they danced to avoid one another's desperate jabs. Felix laughed.

When two men went for the trustworthy teachers guarding the main doors, Kate intercepted them, exposing brain with a single bash at one and caving in the chest of the other. She reminded Felix of a mythological goddess he'd read about, maybe in one of her classes.

The chaos subsided. Bodies littered the floor. The trustworthy teachers looked traumatized, but they also looked to Felix for an indication of what to do next. The survivors from the brawl, four of them, all men, lined themselves up in front of Felix, each of them with a severed head held by the hair and a steak knife held by the handle but pointed down. They bowed.

Seeing how messy the men had gotten made Felix realize that he'd likely left the pregnant women's dwelling splashed in their blood, soiled again, which might have contributed to people's reactions to him—but these men, holding the heads of their co-conspirators like talismans to ward off death, didn't look more imposing because of blood on their skin. They just looked pathetic.

Felix called the trustworthy teachers closer, and he explained to all that a renegade faction of True Sons had spawned a pernicious rebellion in the Settlement, and their job, now that they had purged all the teachers affected by the blight but these four—meaning the men holding the severed heads—was to proceed with what Father needed done at the school. The school had to be purified, and through its purification, they would be purified.

The schoolteachers, even Kate, looked puzzled.

"Even these four traitors can be saved, but those too much under the influence of the rot are past saving," Felix said. He imagined going from bed to bed, cradle to cradle, but he wouldn't. They would, and in doing so, they would prove themselves. Felix would observe. Felix would *administer*.

"The children," Kate said, no fervor in her voice. "He means the children."

"The students," Felix said. "We can't let rot spread through false teaching. But also... the rest, yes."

"So... what, then?" One of the four brawl survivors dropped his severed head.

"There were too many of you," Felix answered him. "All in the nursery were under your influence at some time or other. None can be saved."

One of the trustworthy said, "You want to—"

"No," Felix said, "*you* want to. Start with the oldest. Muffle their faces. Slice their throats. Kate, am I right that the kitchen has more knives?"

"Yes," she said, her eyes glazed over.

"Move with speed and caution. Don't give them a chance to resist. You're killing children in their beds, not looking for a fight." Felix nodded at the men and women around him, and they stared back, blank-faced. They didn't disagree. They didn't like their task, but they would do it.

They did, turning white sheets all around the nursery red. Felix watched their progress and didn't mind that some of them wept while realizing the young ones' ends. Many reacted to the void's proximity with grief; grief was an acceptable flaw to be shriven.

The slaughter of the Settlement's children ended at dawn. Felix told the exhausted teachers—including Kate, who'd lost the verve she displayed in her role as Monitor—to fan into the streets, where they could recruit allies behind doors with no masks and realize the deaths of enemies behind doors with masks. The Settlement of Passing and everyone in the Nothing Lands faced the void today.

10. PURIFICATION

It will spread like morning fog.

Too late. Nothing can survive.

"The worthy will slay the unworthy in their houses, as I did—the unworthy are unready, easy to end—and we'll pile bodies in the street and have a burning," Felix said. He imagined the smell. The cooked meat of the brothers and sisters that were.

Father sighed a sigh Felix had heard before. It didn't convey sadness, disappointment, or even resignation. The sigh sounded distant, dreamy. When Father sighed, he looked somewhere his eyes couldn't see. "I told you I chose you," he said, placing a clean hand on Felix's messy shoulder.

Had Father told him? Or had Father said he needed to choose *someone*? "What?" Felix said. "Why?"

"I knew you would be incorruptible, impervious to the blight."

Felix slipped the bowie knife from the side of his cinched pants. "Let me cut it out, Father. I'll cut out the rot." He thought of Marianne, cutting baby boys and girls out of terrified mothers. That old battleship would help him fight the rot. Father had an army to command. Felix hoped being *chosen* meant playing general.

Leaning close, lowering his voice to a whisper by Felix's ear, Father said, "I have had so many visions. The blight's corruption is total and instantaneous and as inevitable now as death itself, too late to be stopped by the time the rot manifests."

Lowering his voice, Felix savored the warmth of Father's cheek next to his as he said, "What is the blight, Father?"

"The blight is doubt."

Sudden excitement jerked Felix's head back. "They don't doubt you, Father! Not even the unworthy! Fear of you, belief in your power, controlled their actions right up until they met with the void! I refer to the unworthy, who claim not to believe, but do, despite themselves—"

"Belief in me is irrelevant," Father said. "Anyone may doubt me because I am nothing to believe."

Felix should have known Father would say something like that. Even now, Father imparted knowledge, and again Felix had a sense of a surfeit of knowledge, a quagmire, and he wanted to be, with Father's blessing, back in the muddy streets, in a fray of limbs and screaming.

But Father was life, and Father was death, and Felix was blessed, and would be respectful. "What doubt is the blight, then?"

"Doubt of death's omnipotence," Father said, far away, seeing far, far away. "Doubt that death should be life's true ruler, as we have made it here in the Nothing Lands." He didn't even seem to be talking to Felix anymore. "I am compassionate. It will go better this time."

Felix had thought, before, about Father's teachings—their community's religion, if it was a religion—being bullshit, a social adhesive, but he'd never seen a reason not to accept it anyway because it got the part about death's inevitability right, and in the shadow of that monolith nothing was better than bullshit, so bullshit about death seemed like the right bullshit to believe. Death was eternal. Life was a brief fluke. Life offered silly desperation; death offered incomprehensible majesty.

"The madness," Felix said. "The madness of life."

"The madness of the *desire* to live," Father said. "Come with me."

It will go better this time.

Father led Felix from his personal wing of First House to the back, where the labs and the animals were, and outside— to the grow house. Giddiness knotted Felix's stomach as Father punched in a code on a numeric keypad to open the main door. A feeling akin to exaltation lifted one side of his mouth as they went through a small corridor and entered a plastic airlock—plastic on the floor, plastic on the ceiling, plastic on the walls and on the doors that made sure the atmospheric gases, humidity, and temperature were carefully regulated.

Felix had studied chemistry, but he hadn't gotten far with botany, so he didn't recognize most of the plants in the grow house's first chamber, but he guessed they provided ingredients for what Salvador had called Father's "concoctions." Different types of lamps covered most of the ceiling, but the walls had diagrams and whiteboards with formulas on them, and Felix knew some of the symbols and equations, but it all looked far beyond him. He hoped he would have an opportunity to learn. Was wanting to learn—wanting a future in which to learn—the same as a desire to live? He hoped not. If he died, he died, but if he happened to be alive, he wanted to know...

...to know...

Father's secrets.

Too late. Nothing can survive.

They passed through the first chamber and through another airlock into a second without slowing. Father had a destination in mind, and whatever his instructional intentions, a tour of the grow house didn't figure into his plans. Most of the plants in the second chamber were flowering, reds, yellows, oranges, pinks, blues, purples, a stunning array of blossoms that probably had names.

The third chamber was biggest and seemed devoted almost entirely to mushrooms, some of them huge, some of them like small caps you might find in a soup. Felix stopped to examine a blue one the size of his fist that had what looked like thick white hairs all over its rounded cap, and Father halted in front of him. "Don't touch that one, or anything," he said. "That one secretes an oil that will eat through your skin."

Felix pulled away from the little monster and caught up to Father, who neared what seemed like the chamber's end, an area where, instead of plants or fungus, tables with tanks, hoses, and a computer marked the perimeter. Most of the smaller hoses connected to a larger hose that ran up through a ceiling—ventilation.

"When you said it was too late," Felix said as Father took the chair in front of the computer, "did you mean the blight—the doubt—has spread to everyone?"

"Everyone but you, Felix." Father didn't look at him as he spoke. Father typed. The bases of the tanks, which had liquids in them, hummed, and lights blinked.

Was Felix without doubt if he believed everything was bullshit? How well did Father know Felix's mind? Did Father want to know? What mattered more, knowledge or belief?

Father believed in him. "No one can survive," Felix said.

More typing. The liquids bubbled. "The fog comes in on little cat feet," Father said jovially.

"What?" Before, when Father had mentioned morning fog, Felix hadn't asked, but as the liquids in the tanks turned to vapors, and clouds migrated through the tubes—

Too late. It will spread like morning fog.

Not the blight, or the rot, spreading. Too late to stop that. The antidote would spread with the daylight.

"You sealed the ways in and out of the Lands?" Felix asked.

"Not necessary," Father said. He stared at the computer screen, no longer typing. On the screen, a percentage count climbed upward while a horizontal blue bar grew. "Felix, do you see that safe on the shelf?"

Felix looked where Father pointed and nodded while he tried to understand *not necessary*. Should the blight not be... contained?

"The combination is 1-4-7-5. Go open it and bring back what you find."

In the safe Felix found a large envelope and two masks he could identify from television shows, masks from another reality than the blighted ones' symbolic tragedy masks, rubber and plastic instead of ceramic, yellow and smooth around the face, clear covering for the eyes, bulky pieces in front of the mouth and along each side of the jaw, and with the bulky pieces were what looked like compact power sources for the—filtration—they were gas masks—

ventilation

The tubes coming from the tanks full of bubbling liquid pumped clouds toward the main tube connected to the ceiling.

The fog comes in on little cat feet.

Through tinted windows, Felix saw cloudy wisps tumble from the grow house's roof to the ground outside. He remembered the stories about how the True Sons of the Father that was had met their ends. They screamed about rot. They used anything they could find to cut parts of themselves away. Screams. Felix's ears had cultivated a taste for screams.

He brought the envelope and the masks and set them on the table next to Father's computer. He didn't know what to say. He hadn't been chosen as Father's heir. He'd been chosen to live. Was that an honor when death was the only thing worth living for?

"Put on your mask, Son," Father said. With his short hair, clean cheeks, and lean muscle, Father seemed too young to call him Son. Father was father of all... but Salvador was dead... and Felix could be... something else.

Father shook his head. "Put it on, flip the switch by the left ear, and make this sacrifice for me: carry on."

Little cat feet. Soon, everyone he'd ever known would be dead. He didn't know how to feel. Happy?

It will go better this time.

"Put it on," Father repeated.

Figuring out how the black rubber straps worked took a few seconds, but Felix got the mask situated over his face, secured it around the back of his head, and flipped the switch, which made the filters hum.

"Give me your bowie knife," Father said.

Felix didn't want to. He wanted to convince Father to put on the second mask. The existence of two masks, however, brought a different scenario to mind, one without him, one with two lovers slaughtering the Settlement and taking off together to live in luxury and—

Felix gave Father the knife, and Father handled it lightly as he stood, saying, "In the envelope is everything you need to create a new place when you're ready, a place free and safe from the blight that took this one. You know the outside well enough to use the information in that envelope to find people who will help you, get you everything you need. When you're ready."

"But Father, I—"

"Take time to purify yourself, then go. Let this place fall into oblivion."

"But Father, I... I need you."

"But I'm ready, Felix." In a movement too quick to follow, Father brought the point of the bowie knife to the side of his neck and shoved it in, not slicing his throat but skewering it, maybe even stabbing through his vertebrae, forcing the blade out through to the other side. His eyelids fluttered, and his lips curled upward in bliss as both sides of his neck, knife handle on one side, the point on the other, emitted streams of red. He fell to the side and hit the floor. Felix didn't look at him.

He looked outside, where the fog grew denser and rolled toward the populated streets of the Settlement. He would move with it, helping in its task and, in doing so, be purified.

First, he stripped his bloody clothes, belt included. He left the grow house with nothing but the mask and the envelope. He left First House with the envelope in his backpack and his machete in his hand. He walked alongside the little cat feet. He imagined himself in a wave of feral, hungry cats.

As he and the cats arrived at the residences, he saw no evidence of the blossoming carnage he'd hoped for. Soon, standing over a woman he'd agreed to kill, he would learn that the schoolteachers had tried *reasoning* with the insurrectionists. They lacked the understanding that reasoning with madness was itself madness, which Father had anticipated, seen, and recognized as a form of blight. Yes, too late. Too late before Felix had begun.

Nothing can survive.

Nothing WOULD survive.

When he was ready.

Brothers and sisters that were stood in the streets, roused by news of the planned insurrection or its rout. They gestured wildly, panicked, and many hands held weapons, practical items, kitchen knives and skewers and hatchets and shovels and picks—

and the little cat feet moved in faster than Felix did.

Panicked faces saw him, in his kind of mask, rolling in with the clouds, new shadows in the dapples of dawn.

The fog engulfed them without obscuring them. Felix saw them, they saw him, and they saw each other, and even the sun shone through the morning fog, weak, drunken illumination that somehow made the faces of the brothers and sisters that were look brighter. They beamed through the fog, and their panic melted. The combination of morning sun with morning fog uplifted them.

The man closest to Felix, who held a pitchfork, pointed at him and laughed.

Two women who stood nearby, who had been yelling at each other a moment before, burst into laughter.

The sound came at Felix like an undertow: the wave of cats leapt onto the Settlement and kicked back laughter, resounding mirth.

Felix moved toward the man with the pitchfork. "Please," the man said. "Yes!"

In a fluid motion, Felix dropped his machete and snatched the pitchfork from the man's hand. He stepped back and drove the tines through the man's torso. The man spit blood as he laughed, and he didn't have enough breath to get out a full chuckle as Felix lifted his impaled body into the air and threw it into the dense cloud behind him. As if it were a trident, he threw the pitchfork at one of the paired women nearby, piercing her ample bosom. She staggered with the pitchfork's momentum, staggered back toward Felix, then fell backward, pitchfork wavering but firmly stuck and standing tall.

The other woman covered her mouth but only laughed louder. She looked at Felix, uncovered her mouth, and jumped up and down. "Me next, me next!"

A smell reached Felix's nose and turned his stomach. Rot. He hadn't smelled it in the fog—it hadn't *come* from the fog—it came from the people exposed to the fog. The gas. Father's concoction.

Better this time.

Felix retrieved his machete and looked at the woman, who wiggled and hopped like an impatient child.

"Oh, fuck you for making me wait!"

He hadn't even noticed the long knife in her hand. She pulled it along her throat, making a deep gash. She stopped jumping, but she didn't topple. The hand with the knife sawed at her neck until it spasmed, and her fingers released the knife. Blood poured out of her, and her eyes rolled back, but the smile stayed on her face. She remained upright.

Felix walked by her, into a thickening throng. People buzzed around each other with the same energy that had animated the impatient woman who'd just killed herself. Two young men swung axes at each other. One cut the other's left arm almost completely off, then shouted, "Now you do me!" The other made a sideways swing with his good arm and drove the blade into his... partner's?... side, where he let it stick deep in the gut. "HA-HA! HA-HA! HA-HA!"

The brothers and sisters... the brothers and sisters that were... had never been so *happy*.

Little cat feet pounced before people could see what was happening and react, and the happiness spread to them. What caught Felix's attention first were the people who turned outward, attacking others, asking others to attack them. The "Me next" woman had made him think, for a moment, that he meant something special to the people of the Lands, but he soon observed that many around him would approach anyone who might hurt them with the same enthusiasm.

Nevertheless, he granted requests. A man said, "Please!" and he answered with a swing of the machete to the thigh, not severing the leg but dealing a wound from which the man might bleed to death. He left the man in tears of joy, rubbing blood over his bare body, calling out for a blade.

When a young woman—barely old enough to have missed the massacre at the school—grabbed at his shoulder, he turned, expecting to find more purity in granting her audience with the void, but instead of begging him like the others did, she giggled and bowed her head, the back of which was covered by short, uneven locks of brown hair, pretty in its wildness. "Tell Father I figured it out," she said, and something distorted the way she talked.

"Figured what out?" Felix realized he had to shout over the jubilation of the crowd.

He missed the first part of what she said because she looked up while she said it, revealing the reason for her distorted speech, but as his mind processed the missing parts of her face, including the halved lips undoubtedly responsible for her speech impediment, she finished with "rid of the rot." His eyes drifted downward along her naked body and understood her message. She held a knife, a small one, but it must have been sharp. She'd carved out breast meat and sliced between ribs. Her legs she'd cut in several areas, taking out flesh from the fronts and sides of her thighs and the backs of her calves, but she still managed to stand, which amazed him. The way she took the small knife and cut a deep piece from her forearm as a demonstration for him also amazed him, and the way she moaned while she did it convinced him that the brothers and sisters that were did not feel pain. Father had done more than help them find a way to meet death in their sleep. He had exploded their comprehension, and the explosion of comprehension was ecstasy. They met death in ecstasy.

That most of them were killing themselves finally consumed his notice.

Preventing them from fleeing wasn't necessary because Father had effectively cured the blight and ended their doubt. They begged for death's magnificence and experienced it absolutely.

Felix, jealous, was to be the sole witness and survivor of

their glorious, transcendent mass suicide.

He *could* take off the mask, if he wanted to join them. *Carry on.* Father had wanted it.

And he had unfinished business.

After the demonstration with her forearm, the woman stared into Felix's eyes to hold his attention. Knife in her right hand, she reached down between her legs, where she was already cut and bleeding. As if she were cutting anywhere else, she carved meat that widened her vaginal opening when she pulled it out. Blood gushed, and she giggled, eyes filled with lasciviousness as she seemed to have an orgasm. Felix leaned in to kiss her, but she collapsed before the front of his mask reached what was left of her face.

Probably the blood loss.

He walked through the throng, saw a man smashing a woman with a log while another man stabbed him repeatedly in the back, all of them having the grandest time. After the log squashed the woman's head, the man fell on top of her. The log rolled away, and his back squirted from many gashes, and the man who'd been stabbing him looked down for a moment, laughter fading, until an idea lit up his face, and he jabbed his knife into his eye.

People made a lot of noise, most of it loud, a great deal of it passionate, but none of it screaming, really. Felix didn't know how to feel. Nothing had turned out like he expected. There was severity, yes. Felix had needed Father to be severe... and Father's severity was beyond his imagining. There was also mercy. So much mercy. Felix would not be so merciful, which might mean he would not be as good as Father.

As the Father that was.

Not when *he* was realized as Father.

All around him, people killed themselves, laughing as they cut off their limbs and peeled off their skin and declared victory over rot right up until their moments of death. Orgiastic, ecstatic joy, better than any bacchanalian tasting, and they would all die. Through the genius of the Father that was.

His Father.

He would wait for, and participate, in the suicides, and when all were gone, he would clean the blood from his skin one last time, put on clothes suitable for the outside, and walk away from the only life he'd known. Because life didn't matter.

Thanks to his Father, he had the means to bring his own brand of death to the world. To do what he would with his inherited concoctions, to make more as he saw fit. To build a society with power and reach beyond his Father's vision. The Fathers that had been had never been wrong. Every generation had its own pleasures.

When he was ready to be Father, Felix would make sure his pleasures charmed masses.

ABOUT THE AUTHOR

L. Andrew Cooper

L. Andrew Cooper specializes in the provocative, scary, and strange. Other works include novels and novellas The Middle Reaches (a series), Alex's Escape, Noir Falling, Records of the Hightower Massacre [with Maeva Wunn], Crazy Time, Burning  the Middle Ground, and Descending Lines; short story collections Leaping at Thorns, Peritoneum, and Stains of Atrocity; poetry collection The Great Sonnet Plot of Anton Tick; non-fiction Gothic Realities and Dario Argento; co-edited fiction anthologies Imagination Reimagined and Reel Dark; and the co-edited textbook Monsters. He has also written 35 award-winning screenplays. After studying literature and film at Harvard and Princeton, he used his Ph.D. to teach about favorite topics from coast to coast in the United States. He now focuses on writing and lives with his husband in North Hollywood, California.

BOOKS BY THIS AUTHOR

Alex's Escape

Fourteen-year-old psychopath Alex Packard has his own house, a shadow version of his parents' house that THEY helped him build. He takes people there to kill them in the most entertaining ways he can imagine. After murdering his parents, he moves to Los Angeles to live with his married gay uncles, Bruce and Aaron. Alex bonds with his uncles immediately, coming out as gay, too. His bond with Aaron, a documentary filmmaker, tightens as he shares in Aaron's passion for the camera, and he toys with both uncles, trying to ignite other passions. Meanwhile, he starts bringing beautiful boys and girls from school back to his house, staging more and more elaborate and violent scenarios with them to entertain himself as well as THEM... but his uncles have suspicions, and Alex leaves clues... and Alex might not understand the enormity of the forces that allow him to slaughter innocents in a shadow world.

"Alex's Escape is pitch-black coming-of-age nastiness that delights in every transgression a hardcore horror fan could dream... and several more besides!" - Ryan Harding, Splatterpunk Award-winning author of Transcendental Mutilation and Genital Grinder

"A queer phantasmagoria of torturous horror, taboo sex, and supernatural cruelty. Alex's Escape penetrates deep — in all manner of ways." —Jonathan Butcher, author of What Good Girls Do and Splatterpunk Award Nominee for Something Very Wrong:

A Collection of Lurid Body Horror

"The most twisted and disturbing book I've ever read, in the vein of Barker's best." —David-Jack Fletcher, award-winning author of Raven's Creek

The Middle Reaches (Series)

The Middle Reaches, a four-volume series, tells the story of a place, The Middle Reaches, that connects our reality to another, and in doing so it creates a bridge for monsters to enter our world and for people who venture through The Middle Reaches to enter a world of monsters. The story begins when five friends re-enter The Middle Reaches, barely remembering their experiences there as teens when their friend Sheldon disappeared. As their story seems to close, a new story, about adolescent Bobby Lightfoot on a collision course with a fiend called The Man in the Grinning Mask, intertwines with the original story as a new group of teens tries to catch up with Bobby's legend. After a cataclysmic conjunction, the plot spins forward with gods using monsters to create catastrophe that Bobby and allies try to prevent. The story concludes with a supernatural war the apocalyptic resolution of which requires the cooperation of characters from throughout the epic tale.